VISIT BY MERCIAN MAMA SANJO

BY

DR. ALHASAN SISAWO CEESAY, MD

FIRST PRINTING

PUBLISH KUNSA.COM

INSCRIBED TO

My Parents, Wife and Children, Teachers, Friends,
Colchester Friends of Manding Charitable Trust UK and
Friends of Manding Alpena, Michigan, USA and the
downtrodden.

Many a scientist remiss about having chance to chat with
an alien from afar and visit of Mercian girl Mama Sanjio
just fulfilled that yearning for the Panyeki villagers of
yester years.

Dr. Alhasan S. Ceesay, MD

PREFACE AND ACKNOWLEDGMENTS

This work is a fictional story told many times by my late Grandma Sala Hati Sey. It was riveting and kept us and other village children glued to her until she finishes telling the story of Mama Sanjio, the rain child from space's visit to Panyeki village, Badibou, the Gambia, West Africa.

It reveals how every society had its ideas of planetary people, commonly called Martians, and we see today how much NASA is spending on space adventures not only seeking minerals, but finding out if life or other people like us leave in space. As it stands we know of only human and animals on earth and no where else is there life in this form and use of intellect known to man.

Some argue that a Mercian may be lot brighter than us humans but that remains a fib until proven right either through encountering a Mercian or the revealing of their capacity that excells us. Artificial intelligence mimics fable space creatures but the people of Panyeki and Famori villages some thousands of years ago can attest to the gentle landing of space girl (rain child) onto their fields, who changed their lives forever.

Your appetite being whet I would let you browse through the story in this work. In the mean time kindly allow me express profound gratitude to my wife Mrs Fatou Koma Ceesay and our children: Famatanding Ceesay and Roheyata Ceesay; for bearing through with me in thick and thin during my drive to bring medical aid and service to villagers.

Also I am immensely thankful to illustrious lawyer Ousainu Darboe, Lorna Robinson, Keith Robinson, Eliza Jones, Dr. Laurel Spooner, Dr. Barbra Murray, Dr. Phil Spooner, Dr.

Richard Murray, Dr. Malkaight Singh,Cloyd Ramsey, Kalilu Singateh, Howard Riggs, Rita Riggs, Dr. Charles Egli, Dr. Cooper Milner, Dr. Nelson Herron, Deidre O'Leary, Margaret Cruise, Bill Cruise, Alison Cruise, Dr. Eunice Kahan, Dr. Betzabi Alison-Prager, Henry Valli, Fr. John Milner, Homer Shepard, Geraldine Shepard, Dr. Lamin J. Sisay, Dr. Sulayman S. Nyang, Bishops Masson & Coleman McGhee of the Episcopal Diocese of Michigan, Detroit, the Ceesay Committee Diocese of Michigan, Lois R. Leonard, Rev. Walter White, Rev Huge White, Patricia Koblynski, Ishfaque Ahmed, Ahmed Nizami, Abdinnisir Sequlle, Faisal Alim, Noora Sequlle, Mahmud Adam, Mohamed Nasir, Ganem Al Hadied, Yusuf Ali, Dawud, Ahmed, and numerous others whose names are not mention but not forgotten. I write to raise money for the building of a village hospital at Njawara, the Gambia.

It is my hope that you would be inspired to join our dream of providing medical aid and service to villagers and children. Purchasing this book or donating in cash or kind would help bring our dream to fruition of Manding Medical Centre for a much needed healthcare delivery and hope to villagers, especially children who frequently die prematurely from childhood diseases because of lack of medical service.

Together we can catch a dream for the villager and children. Log onto our website: www.friendsofmandinggambimed.btck.co.uk or www.publishkunsa.com to learn more about our self-help village health project Manding Medical Centre at Njawara. Portions of proceed from sale of this work go to support goals of Manding Medical Centre.

In addition the Centre will in due course offer scholarships to rural candidates wishing to read for a medical or an agricultural degree and return to serve us.

Dr. Alhasan Sisawo Ceesay, MD

Chapter 1

ARRIVAL

Once upon a time; long time ago and at Panyeki village of Badibou Kunkudou in Gambia the firmament was said to be suddenly blanketed by pitch darkness from a huge cloud that covered almost 100 miles long by 40 miles and spread as far as the eye could see and mind envisage.

With pitch darkness whose length is only broken on and of by colourful, rainbow like lightening left people wondering what the signal from the skies was all about.

The phenomenon prompted well respected oracles to warn the coming of one that would rule life and death and that the populace need repent before its arrival. On the other hand master witches contrarily proclaim the darkness to be omen of the coming of a girl that was soon to descend from the darkness to brighten lives of the beleaguered.

People for a while argued about the veracity of the two observations put before them by folks they turn to for solution as a last resort. Most tend to believe the witches for their message was of redemption and not of damnation as predicted by the mighty oracles of the day.

The chief witch told the crowd, "I Wutu Nyimila dreamt of the arrival of a rain girl call Mama Sanjio, meaning girl of the rain, last night and what we see matches it. She showed me the ladder that would be lowered from the skies before she finally appear in human form." The Oracle angrily protested and lambasted the chief witch for trying to deceive the people to gain recognition.

He said, "Do not listen to her. It is her way of bamboozling you through sheer lairs to have you honour her and the likes of her." The old adage rivalry between witches and African oracle took centre stage with the prediction of the coming of the rain child. Hence, it was on this miraculous day of rainy July some hundreds of thousands of years ago that proved the chief witch right.

Hurricane winds of 75 to 200 miles per hour blew over the region in a matter of seconds but destroyed no property. This alone was a phenomenal sing for huts do not; I repeat do not withstand winds at 30 miles per hour more over such ferocity as one that accompanied coming of the rain child.

However the lightening and gale force winds frightened both man and beast to cause them to hide in caves, behind big boulders and trees they deem safe to be at. The wind raged with rain pouring cats and dogs flooding millions of acres of farmland and with it the people saw a silver ladder being slowly descended from the heavens in that fracas of mother nature.

Not until 11:00 pm before the ladder touched down on one of the fields now dubbed 'Tonya Lung' meaning the day of truth. Within an hour of the ladder touching mother earth, an angel like figure in a woman's body took its first step towards the Garden of Eden. One could hear hymn and chants all around her but the choir was invisible.

She made her madden descend in total silence while overwhelmed and frightened humans watched every moment of it wide eyed. Halfway on the descent she stopped and looked up waving and gave a wide rimed smile before she continued her sojourn to mother earth. Some believed she was saying her farewell likewise assuring her parents up in the celestials that all was well and quite safe for her to meet barbaric humanoids. Another hour past before she set her loving slender feet on the ground.

And as soon as she stood free of the silver ladder it vanished upward in spectacular fashion leaving a trail of bright flash skyward. At first no one knew what to do or how to approach the visitor from the heavens or even what to say to her. They wondered whether she would understand any of their myriad languages as was common in such a gathering.

It was the sky guest, Mama Sanjio, who broke the ice by saying, "Hello, I bring tidings from heavenly space and it's a delight to touch down on this tinny rock of yours. I came in peace and ready to help you." Her soft unobtrusive speech stunned and petrified everyone for almost ten minutes before seven year old girl, Sutuknug Foro, walked forward and held Mama Sanjlo's hands and curtseyed and said, "My name is Sutukung Foro but most call me Sutu and I too welcome you on behalf of mankind.

Our home and food is all yours. We will have you as guest of honour and will provide you generosity to the best of our endowments. Do you by the way have a name, brothers and sisters like we do on earth? How old are you?" Mama Sanjio smiled and responded, "My name is Mama beautiful Sanjio. Friends call me beautiful. Up there we have no mums and dads as you have down here on this rock. Up there two people just wish for a baby and it's granted instantly.

Thank you for belling the cat, my dear brave one. No, we are not aggressive but I am warned about the lowness and barbaric nature of man. I come in peace to help you out of that attitude you have towards each other. To do this man must be willing as well as ready to swallow the bitter pill of truth and to reconcile amongst them."

This frank exchange between the brave innocent minded Sutukung Foro and her celestial guest set the preamble of what was to come sooner than later from this phenomenon before a swoon crowd. Difference just revealed by the rain child astonished the onlookers and made them expect more enigmatic stories making everyone move closer so as not to miss a word uttered by the sky guest.

Tradition has it that the village head host the visitor and this made Mama Sanjio his honoured guest that he must provide worthy place and food for her. Luckily food was of no problem for these sky lives do not eat. The rain slowed down to a trickle of fifteen miles per hour as soon as Suntukung and Mama Sanjio walked hand in hand towards home of the village head.

At first there was a hush, hush about this visitor for people did not know what would happen next. Meanwhile war mongering men warriors armed themselves to the teeth in readiness for an unexpected eventuality. Many surmised that the spacemen were about to cease earth for themselves.

However the genteel nature of Mama Sanjio quelled all fears and the possibilities men dreamt of about reason why this soft landing. Soon the Tabulaa, the African talking drum, was struck causing all neighbouring villages and hamlets to converge onto Panyeki Kunda to find out what happened and why the summon. It was not until when most of the village heads were assembled did Suntukung Foro and Mama Sanjio surfaced. Suntukung was first to speak. She said, "Last night our village of Famori was blessed with arrival of the rain child, one from the sky. She and I had few cordial exchanges and do not be surprised to find her being a multilingual. We are definitely friends and I assure you that you are in no danger as she only came for our own good

I was amazed how fast she found our varied languages so easy. My uncle the village head and residents of Famori are pleased to introduce stunning Mama Sanjio from far, far above us." A girl in the crowd asked, "What is your real name Miss alien? Mama Sanjio smiled and replied, "Beautiful, they call me and yours?" The girl replied, "Musu Koyo, but you can call me Musu." An instant friendship ensued between the two.

The scare crow boys were quite for they were not sure what to make of this petrifying enigma before them nor were they going to embarrass themselves should the alien be offended by approaches from men. A third girl asked, "Do not your people have last names like us?" The visitor wondered why second or surnames meant so much to these humanoids. Mama Sanjio looked lost and remained silent for a good minute before asking Suntukung to clarify.

Suntukung Foro told her in her society people are given names and surnames of family linage. It was then that Mama Sanjio said, "Mine is Mama Beautiful Sanji but up there everyone calls me Beautiful. Up there we do not have mums and dads as you have here. In my place one just has to wish and it's approved instantly.

There is an obvious difference between heavenly custom and yours." On noticing interest of the crowd Mama Sanjio raised her voice for all to hear and yelled, "Greetings to all and I am happy to be your guest. I am from planet LOVE where no one needs food or water and above all no aggression exists in our world. We are all one and stand for each other's good.

I came down out of curiosity from celestial contact your rock had with ours some 2000 years ago. The flickering lights and stream of moving white and red lights at night drew my fancy and gave such fascination to cause me to want to experience your world. Hence, the reason why I dropped by is to have a personal feel of it and get first hand information about humans while I help you out of aggressive behaviour.

Believe it or not everyone up there send you greetings and love. They have asked that I tell you of their readiness to join me to help you live a peaceful coexistence instead of the cutthroat relation you now have." This statement took everyone by surprise as it revealed how much their guest from the skies knew about humans and their greedy operations.

Mama Sanjio continued thus, "On top of that we noticed one very bad vice you have. I believe you call it money. You even blame it to be root cause of all evil on earth. I promise you that by the time of my return back to sky Dom you will have a totally new value that allows sanctity and celebration of life instead of the current wanton wasting of it as record of decades of industrial indoctrination and warfare showed."

Mr. Sisawo Ceesay, Father

Village heads noticing kindness radiating from the sky girl reciprocated in manner very common of African treatment of visitors or foreigners. They poured praises and appreciation for her dropping by and assured her that their homes are hers and she should feel free to visit and chat with anyone she likes to talk to.

The gathering having now relaxed and being curios to learn more retired home only hoping to have a one to one chat with their friend from space. Mama Sanjio was even invited to attend most of the Bantaba meetings, place equivalent to or akin to city hall, so that many would have chance to speak with her. This she obliged and was scheduled to attend that to be held on Friday that same week at Famori her host village.

Dr. Ceesay at wilslow Rd, Manchester, UK, peddling to raise funds for Manding Medical Centre Proposed hospital for the villagers...2007

Chapter 2

AT THE BANTABA

The Bantaba is location, mostly either at the center of the village or its entrance where people attend meetings freely. It serves as a seat of village government where villagers air their views on topics to be debated or decided upon by the elders. A decision made here governs all present and absent residents of the concern village or hamlet. It serves as the ritual forum of village jurist purists.

The Bantaba also doubles as an open village classroom to which everyone participates freely making the village pulsate.

It also serves as hall of entertainment during wrestling seasons and in major festivities marking marriage ceremonies. At Panyeki village the Bantaba doubles as an international forum where Senegalese neighbors meet Gambian counterparts. The big sprawling tree at the Bantaba has witnessed thousands if not millions of village meetings and also out lived most current Famori residents.

It proudly celebrates its 150 years of existence. In every village and hamlet an area in the village is normally chosen and designated as the meeting place to discuss affairs of the village or hamlet to which everyone participates in debate and ceremonies through years of its existence.

Here is what a village Bantaba effectively stands for. In Western jargon it simply means the village town hall. The Bantaba is usually located under the shades of a spreading huge mango tree or cotton tree. It is the place where resident of a village chouse to meet, discuss affairs of the community and seek shelter from sweltering heat from the sun.

It is a place to assemble, have conferences, or just to have a friendly talk with fellow villagers. Here villagers make decisions and resolutions and recount history during gatherings at the Bantaba beneath the great tree. History narrated here keeps knowledge of the tribes alive and united. The Bantaba in some villages double as a village classroom to which everyone wishing to attend dose so freely.

The Banataba serves as seat of village government where the heart of the village pulsates. Villagers eagerly and willingly participate in the communal life debates. These may be about land ownership or conflict and dispute are jointly resolved unanimously according to traditional tribal rules.

Hence, it was at such a place that sages and other respected speakers address or lecture their audiences. Residents are cordially invited to attend, participate as well as air their views on a topic or decision. Villagers eagerly and willingly participate in the communal life debates affecting their region.

These may be about land ownership, or conflict and disputes are jointly resolved unanimously according to traditional tribal rules at no monetary cost to those involved. It is at such a place Mama Sanjio found herself inundated with enquiries of all sorts.

This time it was proud Famori village head (Alkalo), Sambu Kunma, who introduced the agenda of the day amid curious onlookers. The village swelled to three times its capacity by the time the meeting started and more and more as far as Senegal poured into Famori to witness presence of wonder from the skies. Right after the offering of prayers, which sounded gibberish to Mama Sanjio,

Alkalo Sambu Kunma got up and said, "I have the great privilege and duty to present gift from higher above to us. Our noble guest Mama Sanjio, nature of whose arrival is now no secretes to any here will speak as well as take question from you in any language." He paused to let it sink in and said, "Yes, in any language known to you. She speaks it more poetically and fluently than any present.

I personally tested depth of her knowledge about humans and was amazed at stories that occurred eons upon eons ago that she tells as if it happened today. She is phenomenon that is sent to help us love each other and stop being deceitful and barbaric towards each other. I do not intend to take your time but do ask that we first deal with urgent matter of case between Jarga Bah and Fafanding Kinte in regards to alleged damage his cattle did to Fafanding's crops."

He then told Jarga Bah, "It is alleged that your animals strayed into the fields of Fafanding and ate or destroyed half of his crop. Upon being told, you denied that it was your animals that did the damage. Is this true account of the story or have you been misrepresented in narration?" Jarga Bah looked straight into the Alkalo's red eyes and retorted, "How long have you known me and have I ever denied what my animals did to any for all these years you were head village?

On my being told I called all the farmers who were said to have seen the cows and none of them was able to say if the animals belonged to me or were just there from another herd. I even made it my duty to get the next cattle ranch owner to come and see if the animals in question were his but he too categorically said they were one coming from far away herds whose owners might be looking for them.

Jarga Sowe is here to attest to the fact of him being at the fields with me when my attention was called by Mr. Fafanding."

Mr Jarga Sowe stood and told the gathering that he and indeed Jarga Bah were at the field to identify the cattle causing damage to Fafanding's farm.

He told the gathering, "I have been on several times to Jarga Bah's heard and have at times helped in delivering some of his calf to point that I know most of them and by markings we placed on them. Hence it would not take a minute for me to tell if those animals belonged to Jarga Bah or coming from some were else. I am certain as now or then that the animals were stray ones and those that destroyed the crops did not belong to any of us before this gathering."

This said Jarga Sowe returned to his seat while Fafanding was asked to put his case before his peers. He was told the two that had just spoken were respectable herdsman that cooperated fully well with everyone since he knew them as young fellows.

Fanfanding went for the jugular and asked that if Jarga Sowe and Jarga Bah have not been caught discussing the case by Lamin Tonya Fola. Tonya Fola was immediately asked to clarify the statement to be true or not. Tonya Fola, "It was late Friday evening on my way to Sabaa and walking behind the herds' men I distinctly heard them discussing on how to baffle the case against Mr. Jarga Bah.

I swore that the conversation related to Fafanding as they did mention the name Fafanding on three occasions before turning to look back; when they saw me they changed the tone of the conversation to Jarga needing to sell some of his troublesome animals to the butchers."

This made the crowd angry and to demand that Jarga Bah and Sowe recalled and tell the truth or face severe penalties for lying to their peers. The Rain child remained quite throughout the debate. Also she was sort of taking note of way humans settle disputes. She asked herself, "Will it end in brawl as she read from many recording about humans?"

The meeting continued and soon the two Jargas were found to be indeed right that they did visit the field and did tell Fafanding that the animals in question were none of theirs. Jarga Bah told the gather the conversation Tonya Fola narrated was misrepresentation of what they were talking about.

Both said Fanfadings' name came up when they felt that he does not deserve such bad luck destruction of his field. They even volunteered to check the other herd fifty miles away to see if they can locate the person to compensate Mr. Fafanding.

They were pleased to ask the head village of Sare Boido whether he and they had not confronted the Jarga at Sarebojo about waste his animals are causing to farmers with them being blamed.

The village head of SareBojo testified that he did join the two herds' men to meet with Jarga Jallow, who reside in the same village with him.

He told the gathering Jarga Jallow did come to him two days before the arrival of Jarga Bah and Sowe with complain that he is missing some of his animals and was afraid they might be snatched by cattle wrestlers. This led the crowd to apologize to both Jarga Bah and Sowe but demanded the head of Jarga Jallow for knowing and having ignored waste his animals caused to farmlands' and crops.

The Alkalo got up and said he and elders were satisfied that Jarga Bah and Sowe were telling the truth and that none of their animals could be responsible of damage done to Fafandings' crops. Hence it is decreed that Jarga Jallow compensate buy paying the amount of D800, 000 plus two healthy cows to be given to Fafanding. In lue of which most of his herd would be sold and money due Fafanding rendered him while Jarga Jallow serve a prison term of no less than five years concurrently with hard labor.

Jarga Jallow was advised that he has an option to appeal against the decision at the divisional Commissioners' court forum. He was reminded that loosing the appeal triples all penalties lived upon him. Jarga Jallow, thought over the decision and in dead silent crowd said, "From what has been revealed by honorable men I do humbly accept the penalty arrived at by this village council of elders.

My sincere apologies to Fafanding for any inconvenience my animals caused him and his family. I repeat I am very sorry and will comply by your ruling." Well, the village meeting having ended amicably everyone turned their attention if not their eyes towards the sky girl who had been very quite throughout the Bantaba exercise at Famori village. First question came from Pate Njie, one very skeptical about celestial life.

He asked, "Child did we hear that your love planet came close to ours some 200 years ago making you enamored with place you recognized as 'Planet Rock'?" Mama Sanjoi asked to be allowed to analyze what procedure she saw and its primitiveness before answering to question posed by Pate Njie.

She said, "How come such a simple case took such wrangling between humans? Were they not able to see the animals coming from Sare Bojo to Fafandings' farm?" She told them had it been Love planet such matter would take no more than three seconds as the events and evidence were obvious for all to see.

In answering question posed by Pate Njie. She to the amazement of crowd not only told him his own age but that of many of his linage going as far back as three generation of Pate's great, great grandparents. That muted Pate but was followed by the oldest oracle man. He teased her saying, "If you are who you said you are why do not you demonstrate some miracle to convey your intentions for us."

 This put off Mama Sanjio but she knew that was the way of man's limited knowledge operates and pomposity. Hence she asked all to turn east and look into the firmament for just two minutes and tell what they saw. Soon some started yelling having seen angels and God sitting on what looked like a golden chariot never seen by any living soul.

The exercised left some convulsing while others knelt and prayed for forgiveness in being ignorant. One asked, "Are you the last Messiah to redeem us from damnation? Do we need to worship you as we did for Christ? To which Mama Sanjio protested vehemently. She told them, "Were I came from no one there worships the other.

Everyone was equal. The question of Deity is of earthling conjecture. No one should ever worship or create worshiping place in my name or in recognition of this visit. We deal with reality and not by advice of oracles." A lady asked, "How can you make us love as well as be forgiving knowing the over zealousness of man?" Mama Sanjio smiled and replied, "That is what exercise you and I will pursue this week. Actions speak louder than voice. Be ready for an overall change in way you see life and yourself."

The girl followed with a rejoinder that made the crowd laugh. She asked, "Please do you know that everyone here is sitting on an egg for fear of you? She begged saying we are impressed by magic you just did but make us have loving hearts towards each other." Mama Sanjio then instructed everyone present to face his or her nearest person shake their hand and huge them asking for forgiveness as well as telling of their love for them.

On so doing the people felt instant relief from being stressed and became very relaxed, smiling and extremely tolerant of each other. From that day and with that small exercise Mama Sanjio exorcised the devil of hate from the hearts of the villagers and made it possible that they instantly change perception and behavior of others the moment they shake hands with them. Peace spread like virus within few days.

Still at the Bantaba forum, an elderly asked, "Is it possible to make man young through his life in manner like yours? You definite do not look twenty years old more over being well over 200 years as you said earlier."

Mama Sanjio, "Were I came from where life neither ends nor does it change form. You are programmed to change form and to effete. This is irreversible for you are on an upward journey to meet your maker." Another villager asked, "What is the mode of transport from Love planet? What is the makeup of the ladder you descended with?"

This showed mans' endless curiosity and Mama Sanjio was too much of a scientist minded than any. Not wanting to speak or lecture over their heads she told them, "Our skills are billion of trillion years ahead of the most advanced man made technology but the ladder was wind, rain and heat resistant and could carry ten million troupes at a go without a link sagging.

Mrs. Famataning Tarawaleh, mother holding child

I do not wish to be worshiped nor do I permit any hence forth to contemplate such hideous defamation of my mission. I repeat I came to earth because I want to know about your ways and I am happy to witness your judiciary system. The second reason of my coming is that we feel very sorry to see you killing each other for no just cause other than being blood thirsty greedy merciless barbaric.

We want to help you value life and celebrate it than destroy it. Peace relates tolerance couched in shroud of honesty and understanding as key ethos to coexistence" Many, many more questions and answers followed before the village head requested an end to the Famori Kunda's Bantaba meeting for that Friday.

The next scheduled activity for the sky guest was for her to attend a forthcoming wedding ceremony the following Monday at Kerewan, a few miles from Famori village. The fame of this friendly visitor spread as far as Mali, Nigeria, and the entire sub-Saharan region. Hence, by Monday millions upon millions of curios people wandered around in hope of seeing, touching or gaining some insight from the gift from the heavens.

Her presence almost over shadowed the wedding ceremony which she averted by requesting that she not appear until the major formalities were done and over with. She told them that she and her earthling friend Suntukung will show up at the most appropriate time. Suntukung became an instant celebrity even though both she and the rain girl deceits and despised from such superficiality.

Chapter 3

WITNESSED A WEDDING CEREMONEY

Village weddings are the most elaborate way villagers express joy, tradition and continuation of social norms. Rain child Mama Sanjio was guest of honour at the wedding ceremony of Mr. Kebba Njie and Miss Amie Jobe held at Kerewan village.

The event started with the village chief priest offering prayers and the witches warding off all evil possibility that may mar the marriage. This done the drumming, dancing and singing ensued but at the back of everyone's mind was the where about of the miracle gorgeous Rain child of the year.

At the highest moment and crescendo of frantic dancing came Suntukung Foro hand in hand with the most beautiful figurine ever seen by humans. Mama Sanjio's appearance caused an abrupt silence as if someone turned the switches off the people. They all stared in wonderment and awe. The two walked bravely to the middle of the ring formed by the on lookers. There was no pushing or fighting to see her. She was visible to all despite their vantage points.

Some even believed that she was standing on a raised platform. Amid dead silence brave Suntukung Foro greeted everyone present and then said, "My uncle the village head (mayor) asked me to welcome all to the wedding ceremony in process here at Njawara village and in being kind to want to share joyous occasion of Kebba Njie and Amie Jobe who tied the knot this morning.

In addition, I am more than delighted to introduce my friend from the Skies, Mama Sanjio but you can call her beautiful, to be specific, of 'Love planet' who has been generous enough to join us in drive to help us out of some earthly evils such as hate and deceitfulness. Without further ado you are now each allowed to place a question each for Mama Sanjio to answer."

There were no loud speakers but everyone who spoke or asked questions came through loud and clear. The first to ask was one suffering from leprosy. Binta Sonko said, "Beautiful, I have been afflicted with disease that no earthling seemed to be able to cure. Can you remove from me and all afflicted by such disfiguring?"

Mama Sanjio walked straight to the lady and held her, prompting an outcry from the crowd as they fear for her being affected by the disease. Nothing of that sort happened. Instead to the lady's and all present amazement the swellings and multiple disfigurements disappeared instantly leaving the lady looking young and stunning to envy of all ladies witnessing the miracle from space. The entire crowd knelt and thanked Mama Sanjio in deep gratitude.

The treatment erased the disease from all afflicted in the region as well as on the face of earth. For two hours people with complains ranging from rheumatism, arthritis, blindness, Alzheimer, impotence, infertility, relationship problems etc came before Mama Sanjio to be redeemed for good. Like most expected the wedding ceremony celebration became secondary as more and more asked questions. Some initially doubted Mama Sanjio and labelled her a supper magician.

On that she gained instant convert one after another like ripe fruits dropping form a mango tree on a windy day. Twenty hours into the exercise Suntukung Foro leaned towards her friend and in whisper asked if she had enough or dose she wish to limit requests from the people. Mama Sanjio smiled and told her earthling friend that time was only an essence on earth not where she came from and that she would continue helping as long as the people needed.

Both smiled allaying the curiosity of the crowd. Then a blind child led by her mother was brought forward and she stretched her tiny hand out to Mama Sanjio and upon feeling that of the guest's the girl knelt and said, "Mama I was born blind and never saw the face of my parents, siblings nor seen beautiful flowers people describe to me. Can you help me see these things and be your apostle forever?"

Everyone was amazed at the directness and truth in the child's request. Mama Sanjio came closer and said, "Little one, what is your name? The girl replied, "They called me Seyabalo kinte, meaning that which never precious. My parents were kind to love me so much for no name matches mine. What is yours?

Mama Sanjio told the girl, "I Mama Sanjio but from now on you can call me beautiful for it is something both of us share." Seyabalo Kinte smiled on hearing that said of her. Mama Sanjio then asked the girl to imagine seeing the most beautiful roses. The girl did and out from the sky dropped the most beautiful bouquet of red roses which Mama Sanjio handed the girl and then asked her look at what was in her hand at the time. Seyabalo Kinte could not believe her sight.

She not only saw the sun for the first time since birth but those lovely faces of her parents, the bouquet of rose and delightful face of the rain child and the crowd. Seyabalo Kinte thanked Mama Sanjio amidst rapturous applause from the overwhelmed crowd.

Mrs. Binta Ceesay, my elder sister

Seyabalo Kinte thanked Mama Sanjio over and over before hugging her parents in joyous tears bringing a tear or two from everyone present that day joyous historic July day. Everyone was delighted for the girl and grateful to the rain child for love she exhumed.

It was at this juncture that the village head of Famori asked the honourable guest to end the session to allow the festivity of the wedding to proceed. Suntukung Foro and Mama Sanjio soon disappeared amidst cheering and grateful crowd who vow to do all the sky girl requested of them.

Some express desire for her to visit but the host told them that Mama sanjio wanted to just spend two weeks with earthlings before returning, which time they have no influence. The village head promised to ask Suntukung Foro to lean on her guest to beg her add a few more days to her rewarding visit. The crowd joined him in prayer for that wish to happen.

Famatanding Ceesay   Binta Ceesay and Roheyata Ceesay 2017

Chapter 4

TRAVELS

A few days after that earth shaking miraculous work after Kebba and Amie's wedding by the rain girl Suntukung was able to let it known that her friend Mama Sanjio agreed to extend her stay another two weeks to observe politics in operation, race or tribal relations and thing we called religion.

She told the villagers that the rain child has decided to travel to Nigeria to take note of the above. Again many millions more rushed to Abuja before the appearance of the wonder from the blue skies. On the day of her trip to Nigeria villagers saw both Mama Sanjjio and Suntukung Foro take off and glided gently upward towards Nigeria some three thousand miles away.

To everyone's amazement the duo arrived in Nigeria an hour early but remained invisible until ten minutes to the start of the meeting of the people did they dropped gently from the sky above the podium. Their arrival was welcomed with cheers and rapturous applause by the gathering. Abuja had swollen to 500, 000,000 people that day and everyone behaved very well and in the most tolerant attitude ever displayed by these people.

This was the first time a head of state was allowed to address the guest and those in attendance. Hence, Mr. President of the great state of Nigeria got to the podium ready to impress the sky guest. He began with a long rambling salutation to a seemingly endless list of so-called dignitaries of state and village heads. It took ten minutes before he came to the natty-gritty of the day to which he said, "Never did I ever dreamt of ever talking to someone so pretty from the skies without being asked to see a psychiatrist right away." This made the huge crowd laugh except Mama Sanjio who was neither impressed nor did the rain child cared for lexicon in use. He continued, "We are more than delighted to welcome you to our beautiful country and are likewise eager to share time with you.

Madam Mama Sanjio words cannot express delight my people and I have in your giving us some time to teach us about how to live together in peace. Without further ado I now open the meeting and feel free to run it in the most appropriate manner for you. Again thank you for coming to our beloved land." A long silence followed as Suntukung Foro and Mama Sanjio discussed how to make it easy for the millions to have their worries allayed.

Soon thereafter Suntukung Foro took to the podium and greeted all present and added, "Mr. President my friend from the firmament appreciates your welcome note and had asked me to thank you for it. She came to Nigeria, being one of Africa's largest populace, to observe how Politics, governance, tribal and race relations operate on earth.

To that end she asked that relevant questions be directed." She ended her introductory speech assuring the crowd, all of you will understand what her friend says because her voice was normally instantly translated in any language present without use of interpreters.

A rude fellow yelled, "Tell her we do not have a whole month it will take for she would need more that 250 interpreters to cover languages spoken in this great land of ours. Worse there are other tribes from Angola, Congo, and South Africa etc."

Hearing this made the rain girls smile and said, "Hello earthlings can you hear me? The crowd in unison replied, "Loud and clear mama." To this Suntukung Foro told the crowd, "You all heard the questioned posed by the guest in your languages. Shall we now start so as to cover some ground?" An elderly lady in her nineties stepped forward, knelt and first said, "We welcome you to our hearts and homes.

Kindly tell me what must we do to leave in peace?" Again the rain child said peace is found within and not without. Hence I want all to hold hands and face whoever's hand you held and say to that person I forgive you and love you as I did for myself." The crowd did and in few seconds everyone felt very relaxed and comfortable and willing to be their brothers and sisters keeper.

 For the elderly Granny she turned twenty years younger and prettier. The then old lady now turned glamorous young lady again knelt in gratitude and sang loudly for all to appreciate good did the sky child did for her. Many more wanted same fate but the space girl told them to stay put and each will get their reward when in bed that night.

This was her way of crowd control without use of uniform men and women whose presence she rejected. Everything was fever pitch by the time the most contentious topic dealing with tribe let canons loose. Hence the wonder of the skies above had to ask the eldest in the crowd to define tribe to her. Mama Sanjio did remind the gathering that, "Last week I attended your social union at the wedding of Kebba Njie and Amie Jobe. Now I heard what division or types exists amongst you in perception.

In love planet one is only a person and not as fragmented into tribes as I am made to understand. You will be exorcised of such perception at the end of the day." Ninety nine year old Mata Fatajo started by thanking the rain child Mama Sanjio and said, "Tribe according us means the possession of strong cultural or ethnic identity that which separates me or one member of a group from members of another group. The tribe can vary from place to place due to size of it and having no distinction within it. Many of us accept our languages as yardsticks of our tribe."

She was interrupted by the rain child who asked, "That being the case what tribe would you assign me for I speak all languages fluently and so are my folks up there?" The old sage pondered for a while amid a silent crowd. She raised her head and looked straight into the brilliant eyes of the sky entity and replied thus, "It is hard to give direct factual answer without telling you that it is a God given birth right of the individual who sprang from a particular tribe.

However, here is bit about possible evolution of the tribe. Humans being social animals needing others in other to live happily made its members committed to group they belong or perceive to belong. By so doing it kept individuals from wandering or being constantly at fray with other groups. Thus groups with strong sense of commonality and unity are reward in kinship. These rely upon the tribal instincts of their members for their organization and survival.

As for you, fair lady of space, one would designate you a 'universal tribe' as no one speaks all the languages of the billions of people on mother earth nor fit in as perfectly as you did amongst us. The answer depends on each person's birth as well as on the particular tribes that are used as a point of reference - because tribal life itself is not the same for all tribes;

the environment where a tribe lives has an especially important influence." This made the crowd applaud for they too had no answer to define entity that came from the skies which was before them. This was followed by endless competitive definitions from the various tribes assembled. The rain child put a stop to it when it headed no were except repetitiveness and unearthing of old wounds between tribes.

Mama Sanjio said, "Thank you for enlightening me but it seem that you are at lost for want of security that made you huddle in groups instead of accepting and trusting each other , especially those you consider not belonging to your kind. No wonder you constantly yearn for leadership. Do not look down at your social worth just because you think others are not impressed by you or paying attention to you. Self-worth is synonymous to wellbeing. Can any tell me how you govern yourselves?"

This time the president who was quite most of the time jumped in and said, "Madam, I take it that I am the right one to throw light on that aspect of our ways and leadership. In view of the fact many diverse tribes and people exist in a particular country we thought it best for village heads, chiefs, divisional commissioners and a central government ruled by parliament headed by a either a prime minister or a president like me.

Let us start from top towards the bottom of the political hierarchy. In republics the country is led by a president coming from the party wining the majority of vote of the commons. Term Prime minister implies that country is still answerable to king or queen and the privy council of it former coloniser. Every village is headed by one selected by its residents to rule as well as be arbiter in not so serious family or farm disputes among residents. Tradition survives in this fashion. Next are the chiefdoms where all heads of villages select one they want to rule the district they belong. The chief is the custodian of tradition and one that deals with more serious offenses before they get to the western style arbitration at the commissioners forum.

The Commissioner's role is spill over of colonial way of solving local administrative problems and here lawyers wrangle about the rights, innocence or guilt of their client by quoting similar adjudications or mitigating circumstances. When this fails then the case is referred to the central court and later to the country's Supreme Court where any decision arrived at is final and irreversibly binding.

Aside the above various parties under different banners contest place for parliament or local representation. Parliament represents interest of the electorates and makes laws in their name and benefit. The president appoints and heads the cabinet and is head of the executive. Along with this is an independent judiciary which sees to it that fair and equitable open justice is being exercised in the country.

I represent the Peoples Progressive Party and our party having garnered the most votes in the last general election I assumed the leadership of the country, now a republic, as president." The rain child was definitely impressed by his summery but felt that it was all a farce for party or village head systems are liable to tampering and illicit manipulations.

She told the crowd, "Where I emanate everyone is equal and hence no need of this fragmented confused leadership scenario just painted before us.

Had you accepted that mankind is the same needing each other there would not be this emphasises of tribal belonging or party loyalty. What matters first and foremost is to love oneself and then transcend it to the next other person(s) with prejudice of any kind. Your world seems led by two incongruent factors. They are money and war predicate by lust for power.

As your definition stands I am 'musty tribe' but would I be accepted by all the tribes gather hear? Discords by just one of your tribes would throw me into an abyss of confusion and that is what tribalism suffers when people foolishly believe in propping theirs' while subjugating other tribes they do not affiliate with or belong to.

We have no need for party or leadership as there is complete trust in all hearts. You must learn to accept that the other being like you have a temporal time on this rock of yours. The more you cooperate the more for realization of peace would be yours and your kindred's."

Dr. Ceesay and wife Fatou Koma-Ceesay 2000

It was getting very late and the Suntukung Foro and her sky friend were led through throngs of admirers to their opulent palace where they would stay until the open of parliament on Monday being three days from day they arrived. A banquet was thrown for the guests but the rain child ate very little just to satisfy her presidential host and hostess.

At the ball she danced better than any and was very agile indeed. Her nibble feet matched the African rhythm perfectly to everyone's wonderment as if they were born on earth. She never took a gulp of drink of any kind during the whole ceremony. And for this people not only admired her but loved her more. They want to rid off drink and smoke problems but peer pressures and social conditions seems to always nudge these weakling into either smoking or drinking intoxicants or popping drug for leisure.

Mama Sanjio told them that the cause of crime amongst them is due to such bad habits they took for granted. She told them that there was no need to drink to stupor just because one was not willing to be honest and face realities of life. She warned, "Drinking destroys your mind, social behaviour and makes life unbearable for loved ones. Above all your liver cannot stand alcohol and so it becomes destroyed or turns into serious liver disease causing certain debilitating ends."

The evening ended at that sombre note from the skies. People looked at her in awe and whispered she might be the last prophet God was sending to bring order and to calm things on earth before the day of Armageddon. Sceptics even had daring mind to castigate her as one of the jinni wanting to take their beauties with it when returning to its home up there.

Very soon parliament day came and it seemed all of Africa assembled or joked for post to have glimpse of wonder from the blue skies. Flags and buntings of fifty nations were that day raised in each street in Abuja, Nigeria.

With all members of parliament and invited guests seated the presidential limacine drove slowly through throngs of millions of well wishers and on lookers bringing the guest of honour with it. The rain child waved as if a politician and the crowd loved it when she occasionally in the most feminine way through kisses in the air towards the crowd whiles the motorcade passes.

It stopped by the main doors to the parliament and Mama Sanjio, Suntukung Foro and the President stood at attention while the band played the Nigerian National anthem to the delight of the crowd and their guests.

All stood when the president an entourage entered and took their respective seats. The rain child sat next to the president instead of his wife who took a seat behind them. The speaker of the House of parliament dressed in golden attire and of traditional style in nature asked all to be seated.

He then delivered the longest opening speech he ever gave throughout his political career. At the end he said "I now invite our head of State and president of the great people of Nigeria to address parliament and to tease us with good his government intend to deliver in our behalf. Mr. President the floor is yours sir." The president rose amid rapturous clapping from both government and opposition. This day was intended to be that of a unity day for Nigeria.

The president raised his hand and lowered it gently requesting silence to allow him deliver the shortest speech of his political life. He began by greeting the normal line of dignitaries, and VIP guests adorning the chamber. He told parliament that his government intend to make life easier for them and oil has just been discovered at the delta which would rake in plenty of wealth for all Nigerians and would provide more commerce.

In addition he told them that he has commissioned ten thousand tractors to be distributed to places where they would be of more use letting farmers be more productive. He told the gathering, "An empty belly is an unhealthy nation and hence Nigeria should be self sufficient of food and any other natural material such as diversification of hardy crops to ward off effect of destructive hordes of insects and effect of global climate change."

This was welcomed with five minutes standing ovation by parliament to wonderment of Mama Sanjio. She thought what she heard was just bare bone duties of a people and saw no need for excitement portrayed before her. However, she kept her feelings to herself and just confided to Suntukung.

When the applause died down to a trickle the president turned towards the miracle from the skies and said, "Ladies and gentlemen of African realms allow me introduced one that has stormed our minds with such positivist and candour that only her can spell out her love for us.

I heard about this beauty and way she descended to earth three weeks ago and thought that it was only befitting that she grace us with her presence and address this illustrious chamber of African minds.We are grateful to her and Miss Suntukung Foro who had become her best earthling friend and guide.

Without further ado, I now present guest from the skies and most stunning, if not petrifying Mama Sanjio, who by the way you can just call her BEAUTIFUL." Again the whole house stood amidst rapturous applause which deeply touched the rain child's heart. The same response went on in the street as people unable to gain seats in parliament watched over giant television screens all over Africa, Europe, china and the Americas.

It was an instant worldwide event. The cheering took ten minute before it stopped. Mama Sanjio with a smile took centre stage. She said, "I bring tidings to all of you and I am happy to be here to see how you govern yourselves. It reminded me ways we had some millions years ago. Mr. President, people of Africa, you owe to yourselves to love and cherish each other. Your continent is one of the richest on this rock of yours but deceit and hypocrisy mar your ripping the benefits.

One wonders why you do not have one currency, teach a language that all will use through Africa and above all why are your politicians so afraid of its intelligentsias or being original? What was wrong with term, 'Organisation of African Unity'? You rushed to change it to African Union the moment Europe changed from the EEC to the European Union.

This yo-yoing made you not respected by the so-called developed or former colonials. I am here to help and the only way that end can be archived is to point out ineptness in way you do things. For instance why do you fall fool of other regions you falsely designated as developed countries and swallow ala cart whatever they tell or throw at you? Stop being consumers and be inventors and entrepreneurs and most insist on your system to allow others to respect and value it.

On my way to Abuja I saw disgraceful homes in comparison to the one I was lodged. For wealth this country has such disgraceful segregated desperation should never be tolerated. I hope you learn to stand by each other than waving that funny currency of yours. It cannot buy you life or happiness but loving and treating your fellow humans can provide much need and unexpected happiness that would disarm all your stressful ways.

That which you assumed to be power is very temporal and worthless as another can snatch it from you soon than you expected. Money cannot buy you eternal life, true love nor can it guarantee heaven on earth or hereafter. It certainly unravels one's life into your believing that you can, like a drunkard, move mountains and as a result turn morally corrupt or is corrupted by cronies.

Remember to love and respect your ladies through who you descended to earth." The crowd ruptured into dancing, and singing praises to the sky angel. One could distinctly hear the ladies, especially elder ones saying, "Tell them for men have bullied and over ridden us since the days of Adam and Eve."

Mama Sanjio said, "It is never late to turn into new leaf but you must train you mind towards that objective. You must accept you are all humans despite hues and you all share same needs and burden. No tribe or race is superior to the other as nature will never reverse role of the genders. In this life form you exist as men and women and there can never a change to that no matter what social experiments you dream about or may bring to play.

Government most create jobs, provide better housing, allow freedom of the individual, and above all educate the young. There has to be discipline in families and everyone must participate in guiding children toward better future than this free for all drinking , sex, drugs and hopelessness kids engaged in knowing both the security and family look the other way until it becomes too late for the poor child that only wanted their love.

Finally, I would like you turn towards each other and ask for forgiveness and to vow to love each other." There was rumbling through the throngs of people throughout the city and when it died down Miss Suntuknun Foro rose and thanked the government and Nigerian people for inviting both she and her friend chance to attend this august gathering that was about to close.

It was now turn of the leader of the opposition who in brief said, "My party and people will never forget Mama Sanjio's kindness and would put into action all she had outlined for the development of the region and continent. I assure you madam rain child of my party's readiness to work hand in hand like glove with government to bring development and relief to lives of the people irrespective of their abode."

He assured her that his party in conjunction with the ruling party will see to it there are more, schools of all levels, universities, healthcare and good roads throughout the length and breathe of Nigeria. He thanked and took his seat. This was followed by the national anthem and departure of head of state and guest to a luncheon at the people's hall down town Abuja.

The spectacle continued as people laid bouquets of tropical flowers, never seen anywhere except Africa, on roads leading to the great peoples hall. The rain child loved it and at one moment decided to walk and shake hands with the people. Her arrival to the people's hall was delayed by three hours because of this show of love for the people.

Suntuknung Foro became instant celebrity and posed with lot of people and made endless friends on the way. No camera was able to register photo of Mama Sanjio for she thought it bad trophy and mementos to take back to her people.

Dudou Ceesay, Brother with family

Three hours after the luncheon Mama Sanjio and Suntukung were driven through the streets of Abuja for people to serenade them. There were dances and singing inter mingled with poetry in behalf the sky girl and her friend. Many promised to honour the visit by naming their first born after the rain child from the firmament.

As the saying goes good things never last long and the guests were on their way to the airport to return to Gambia. The president and cabinet were at the airport to see the visitors off. And after two hours flight the entourage arrived but Suntukung Foro and Mama Sanjio who disappeared in thin air where at the tarmac before the huge jumbo jet landed at Yundum International Airport, the Gambia.

Cheerful Alasan Mbalow Jr. Sweden 2017

Chapter 5

RELIGIOUS PRACTICES

Having now witnessed both social practices and political operatives of humans the rain child was invited to attend two major religious services representing two faiths that have been on tug of war ever since their inception.

The first she attended was that offered at the Grand central mosque at Njawara on Friday afternoon. Mama Sanjio and Suntukung Foro dressed with requisite attire expected of women attending such Islamic prayers and were seated at a different room at the back of the mosque.

The sermon and prayers of the day by the Imam was relayed to the women via loud speakers. Here along with other ladies they sat patiently waiting for the Qudba and Friday prayers. Soon at around ten till 2:00 PM the voice of the Imam came through the speakers saying, "Verily, Verily, You believers are admonished to follow and practice your faith acidulously. Be not swayed by current trendy and fashion. God and his angels see and know everything one dose."

This was followed by reading of long prayer verses from the Quran and a call to prayer by one of the elders of the mosque. All stood and the Imam say God is great following it with two suras then prostration and placing of the forehead to the ground in complete submission to almighty God. This was done twice before he sat down and did the salaam which the congregation repeated after him.

Mama Sanjio was by the end not impressed with the performance she deemed waste of time. At the end of it she was led to the Imam by one the elderly ladies. The Imam refused to shake her hands but just raised his while carrying a pretending smile on his face.

The child girl noticed and asked, "Why was there no female Imam officiating the Friday prayer with you? Do you know you came from and were nurtured by a woman? Why are men and women segregated during prayers in mosques?"

The questions embarrassed the Imam as it points out the shortcomings of the faith or illustrate unfair treatment Muslim women endure. He politely replied, "Our faith has more respect and love for women than any and that through it they shall be on the right hand side of Almighty God in here after. We do not differentiate people or gender. All are equal and are so treated in the eye of the Mosque.

We do not have women Imams because of the makeup of women and their monthly experiences which could be difficult for them to carry out the day to day functions of an Imam. Any how it was a pleasure to share the Friday prayers with you. What religion do you follow or believe in?"

The rain child laughed and told him, "Religion is an archaic practice people up there would laugh at. None the less I wish all of you the best." Suntukung Foro and the rain child chatted for a while with the ladies before heading back home. Mama Sanjio was not the least impressed but thought it was good way of making human congregate towards a common goal and belief.

Her next adventure was at the grand Cathedral, called St. Paul's Cathedral' located at the centre of the Sare Yarobe town some twenty kilometres away from Njawara village. The whole town was dressed up in crosses of Christ with flowers left at the base of each cross.

The prayer that day was officiated by the Rt. Rev. Bishop Samba Sowe and the very Rev. Fr. James Bah. Along to help were both lay and junior priest, Fr. Dominca Mendy, from other parishes. The pews were packed by the time the rain child and her friend walked into the church building with all eyes glued onto them.

The junior priests started the sermons and prayer before the Rt. Rev. Bishop Samba Sowe got to the podium. He commenced saying, "In the name of the father, holly ghost and the son, I join you to prayer. But first let me welcome our friend from space to the true religion on planet earth.

We follow footsteps and examples of our lord Jesus Christ and are sure to be on the right hand of our father God in life after this temporal one. We would definitely like to know from the rain child if any worshiping is practiced at where she came from. She is whole heartedly welcome to the church of the Virgin Mary and Tabernacle of Christ."

This opening remark was followed by hymns and loud chanting by congregation ready to impress space girl. The Bishop preached covering current world upheavals and also for peace to descend on all earthling in the name of their lord Jesus Christ. To which attendants voiced resounding "Amen!" which made the rain child turn to look at Suntukung Foro's reaction.

She mumbled something that no one heard except her and Suntukung Foro. The prayer was fast tracked for everyone was eager to know if space people believe in religion if so which religion was it. There was a hush when the Bishop closed his sermon with prayer for peace and the well being of all in church and throughout the world. The Bishop and priest stood by the door to give blessing those who took leave to attend other important chores.

A majority stayed and waited patiently to hear the rain child talk to them when she came to the podium. On taking the mike Mama Sanjio with a smile said, "Fellow Parisians, it is a pleasure to be with you and watch you worship. Where I came from you would be seen as kids trying to entertain for believing that there was cake on the moon which would one day drop down to them.

The idea of a superior being is comical and very ancient. However, if it stabilizes your minds and encourages you to be kind towards each other then keep it up. Two day ago I attended one which had different way of worship but in final analysis you both yearn for the same thing only getting to it with very different perceptions to a point you are ready to kill any that differs with your practice.

Hence reason why some ill-begotten minds have hijacked religion for their own selfish ends. We up there noticed too much mayhem and killings done in the name of religion. And what is mind bungling about today's political incursions into religion is that the prophets you purport to follow do not agree with your miss portrayals of theology and use of their name for cruel deeds on earth.

Miss Famatanding Ceesay, Daughter

I admonish all faiths to start preaching against double standards and to encourage peaceful coexistence. None of you ever saw or had a direct telephone call from that which you called Almighty God. Your governments and communities should concentrate on healing rifts and disease amongst you than building toys to float in space.

Again, thank you for inviting me to your service. My people up there would think me coming from dream land when I join them soon. Be happy, trustworthy and above all be a positive contributor to any community you may in due course find yourself. Cheers." This unexpected frank speech left everyone stunned and wide mouthed.

The space girl in just twenty minutes has forced mankind to think again and to look back into their perceptions, believes, and relations towards each other. The truth being a bitter pill was hard to swallow so few disgruntled members complained and lodged charges of heresy against space girl.

Those who met the Grand priest about it found themselves disappearing into thin air never to be seen again. This made both Bishop and Imam, supposed interfaith group of the city, to approach angry rain child and seek clemency on behalf the protestors. She told the delegate to go pray for forgiveness for being part of the falsehood those complainants followed.

Until her return skywards no one had mind to say any bad thing or doubt force accompanying Mama Sanjio. This became part of her legacy for visits to religious organisations. Next human exercise she wanted to observe was the operatives of western style advocacy and ways serious crime was dealt with.

Chapter 6

WITNESSED WESTERN JURIS PURIST

It is said Justice delayed is justice denied. However it must be dispense fairly blind of status of any to be judged. Deceit, greed, and delusional overzealousness for power can prevent dispensation of justice. Today our guest from the skies is invited to sit in and observe the court room at the new Bailey in action. Hence she will be watching lawyers for the defendant and the prosecutor battle it out in court as to veracity of points they put forward on behalf of the defendant or government, in this criminal case soon to be heard.

Being a murder case three judges were selected to hear the case and to guide a jury of twelve men and women who were screened before being finally agreed upon by both prosecutor and defenders. With rumour that the space child might attend the court room was full to capacity before 9:00 AM even though the case was scheduled to start at 10:00 AM that day.

Traffic was stopped as the queen of space rode to court in beautiful dress matched by none. Security was beefed to maximum, with sharp shooters at roof tops of all nearby building and vantage places around the Supreme Court.

There was great fear that friends of the accused might take chance to spirit the criminal away on his way to court while people pay more attention to the enigma from space. All being in place and guests seated the three judges made their entry via a private door to the court room. This being a murder trial, all judges were dressed in crimson red from head to toe and they looked very fearsome lions to behold.

Their entry was announced by the Sergeant of the court and everyone stood until the trio were seated. The chief judge them asked both the prosecutors and defenders of they were ready for start of deliberations with questions and answers about the case. Both teams bowed their heads and replied, "We are ready to precede your lordship."

It was then that the judge asked the sergeant to usher in one to be tried. Soon a six footer very muscular fellow under high escort by arm guards was led to a specially built cage for him to be at during the life of the trial.

He was shackled all over, which he protested against as soon as he saw his girl friend seated in the balcony upstairs. He had nerves and shamelessness to wave and wink at her. With serious looking guards all around the Chief Judge asked the plaintive to tell who he was and what address he leaved.

The man stood and said, "Your honour, my name is Crime Master but children and women called me 'Robin of the Park or simply Rob' and I have no abode except the detention place I came from." The answer angered the prosecutor who rose to make it clear that the defendant before the court had to seen as an aggressive person and enemy of the court and most not be allowed any Calvinistic chances as he had already started.

The Judge told him that his point will be taken into account but he saw no aggression in one giving their identity as the person on triad did. Now he turned towards the defendant and said, "Medical report before me show you in good health and of normal sanity and that you suffer from no deafness.

I now read charges preferred against you by the prosecutor and ask that you agree or deny any aspect as read by me. Do you understand Mr. Crime Master?" The caged man replied, "I fully understand." The judge then started thus, "Charged as follows:

1. You are accused of forcefully entering into the house of the deceased, Mr. Foday Faye on or about 2:00 Am on the night of his brutal end.

2. You are according to witnesses said to pick a fight with the deceased and having used a heave instrument knocked him dead with one blow to the temple.

3. That you then ransacked his place and attempted to set on fire but you were interrupted by the arrival of the securities.

4. You refused arrest and punched an officer who to the present remained in coma at the hospital.

5. And finally you while at the police station continued resisting and fighting all that came your way. Do you agree that all the above took place or not?"

Crime Master looked straight into the red eyes of the judges and said, "I deny killing any one especially the deceased. It was in self defence that caused injury to the police office and am very sorry for him and his family.

Also the police were one who forced a fight onto me for I had my hands up and was about to let them know I found the man dead not long before they were called in. I never killed him, meaning Foday Faye, but the police made me hold the said weapon just to connect or fool me into having my figure prints on the weapon involved in the alleged killing of Foday Faye.

I may have walked onto a brawl and the culprits disappeared on hearing my footsteps. Even the police can testify finding a step ladder used by the escaped criminal. I again strongly deny having caused any grievous bodily harm to Foday Faye or cause his death as charged. I am not one that would or might perpetrate such a heinous act knowingly or otherwise."

He paused and took his seat leaving almost all in balcony believing him. The judge told the clerk to enter that the defendant in a sane state refuted all charges preferred against him by the prosecutor. The case now continues with the prosecution presenting its case or findings against said Mr. Crime Master.

The able prosecutor put on his wide rimed bifocal goggles and sad, "Thank you, your lordship. We shall proof beyond the shred of any doubts that the man before us, notorious Crime Master, in the cage was sole perpetrator of the most hideous brutal act that occurred in this city for a long time ago.

The said crime and murder thereof happened on or around 2:00 Am on Saturday the 1oth of October 2003 at the home of the deceased Mr. Foday Faye, at 12 Ingram Street, Banjul, Gambia. I now call my first witness Mrs. Wahkat Njie who was present and did hear the altercation between the deceased and the said person before the court in-front of us.

The bailiff went and got Mrs. Wahkat Njie, who had her face overly painted and plastered with too much of make to show her social status to viewers. She was asked to hold the Kuran and swear that all she will tell the court about the case will be nothing but the truth so God help her.

Being seated, the Prosecutor smiled and walked gently towards Mrs. Njie and resting one elbow by her table told her, "Miss Njie you just swore to tell the truth to your peers about to pass judgement against the fellow in the cage. Would you in clear simple language tell all of us what you heard or witnessed during the said night of the killing of the deceased Mr. Foday Faye?

First tell us why you heard the noise at such late hour." Mrs. Wahkat Njie looked a bit shaken but started right away saying, "It was around 2:00 AM when I was woken by loud argument between what looked like two fellows. The voices were deep and male like. It made me open my window which is located adjacent to the deceased Foday Faye's door.

I knocked protesting that they were disturbing us and asked if they could wait until daylight to talk it over peacefully. Right then my request was followed by dead silence and the window made a creaking noise. I had someone say, "Hurry up before the door is opened." I now believe that voice to belong to the defendant in the cage.

Afraid, I called my husband to help pry the door while I call police for it may have been thieves who visited the now dead man. Few minutes later the man in the cage appeared from no were and joined us to open the door. With his strength it took no time for the mission to be accomplished.

We walked in darkened room and the accused took a lighter out and lit it for us to see. It was then we saw the horror of what took place moments before my calling attention to the disturbance. I called the police. Shortly thereafter the police arrive and told us that they saw this man, she pointed at the fellow in the cage, running from the building of the deceased.

They had hard time restraining him for they were puny compared to giant they want to arrest. It took three more officers before they could restrain him. I have not seen him stab or hit the dead man nor did I ever saw him other than that night and at this very court.

This is all I knew abort the fatal end of the deceased." The Prosecutor in placing a rejoinder told the witness that she was certain she was not keeping away any other pertinent information that would service justice in the proceedings. Mrs. Wahkat Njie replied emphatically, "No, Mr. Prosecutor."

It was then that the prosecutor in a mocking way turned towards the defence and told them, "She is your witness." The chief defence Counsel walked assuredly towards Mrs. Wahkat Njie and said, "You did impress this court of having good recollections even if they had happened dead at night in a darkened room." Mrs. Njie threw a smile and waited for the time bomb question to follow.

The Defence lawyer said, "Let us for one moment imagine that all you said here was right. Can you tell us your relation with the deceased Mr. Foday Faye?" This question drew fear and raised blood to her brain as it was clear the lawyer was up to no good and might have known her secrete romantic relation with the dead man.

She clenched her fist under the table and replied in a very low suspicious voice, "I knew Mafoday Faye, since high school some years back and was delighted to share a building with him. I had free access to his room and he became good friend of my husband and the two used to fish together.

We were good neighbours and reason why I went to check his door when I heard what seemed men arguing with him." The Lawyer followed by asking, "Did you just tell this court that you heard what seemed to be multiple voices in the same room and night of killing?" "Yes," she replied making the lawyer turn to the judges saying "Your honour court is told by the witness that more than one person was present in that room at the time of the killing.

Would the prosecutor and police explain why they insisted that my client was sole perpetrator of this heinous?" By this time the prosecutor had enough and said, "Your lordship can you bear on the defence to stop harassing the witness? She had told as far as she knew all that which she heard and saw; hence what is this witch hunt all about? She is just witness of the crime not one on trial in this court but the fellow in the cage is."

The Judge intervened warning against court gimmickry as the prosecutor just commenced. It was then that the defence lawyer told the judge that he has at the moment finished with the witness but reserve right to recall her should it be necessary. Mrs. Wahkat Njie stepped down gladly but to her surprise the second defence counsel requested permission to cross-examine her in view of material just brought to the team's attention by their research team.

A copy of the finding was passed to the prosecutor's bench. Despite protest by the prosecutor about admissibility of what was about to be part of the record the judge allowed it be entered as exhibit (A) as well for the defence to cross examine Miss wahkat Njie.

The judge reminded her, "Please take the stand and do not forget that you are still under oath and all your answers will be recorder for the jury to revisit." Nervous Mrs. Wahkat Njie went back to the stand and an unfriendly attorney went straight for the jugular.

He asked her to be truthful and proceeded thus: "Would you kindly tell this court whether you were having secrete romance with the decease, Mr. Foday Faye and that it was not until your husband caught both of you red handed in bed in the act of sex that the two of you agreed to finish him up and weave such fabrication as you just told the court a few minutes ago?"

All Mrs. Njie could say was that, "My personal relations were not on trial but whether I heard noises followed that followed discovery of death a person who leaved next door to my room. I really do not know what you are getting at. My husband and I loved each other and there was harmony between us and the deceased. Why on earth you want to throw such filth onto us?"

The Attorney said, "Your honour, please allow me present exhibit (A) in defence of my client." He first showed the photo to the judges and then gave a copy to the prosecutor who now saw his case unravelling right before his eyes for relying on one that had vested interest in death of the said Foday Faye.

The chief prosecutor being outwitted requested the defence to join him at the judges' chamber for a brief discussion about material he thought not yet ready for public consumption. The judges accepted the request and the court stood adjoined for ten minutes for the law to take proper cause in the case.

Mean while both Mrs. Njie and her husband Abdulie Njie showed signs of uneasiness and braking down causing Mr. Njie to yell "She did it because he was having an affair with Foday Faye for three years before I got suspicious of the relationship between to two when Mrs. Wahkat would bring in a bundle of money from the room across.

At first I thought she was involved in drug dealing for the man which she vehemently refuted. So I told her I would be travelling to Farfeni and would not be back for two weeks. I had a copy of the keys to Foday Faye' room and mine made for me. I kept away from that street for two days to let them feel comfortable being certain of my absence.

It was on said night that at 2:00 Am I decided to trap the two. I opened the door and found them in midstream of sexual act. They wanted to jump but only I was standing right over them. Foday Faye in utter shame covered his face said, "Do with me what must be my fate."

It was she who took the heavy board with intent to hit me but I ducked and it landed on the deceased while he was trying to get up. He fell instantly and was cold right away. My wife de4cided to call Mr. Crime Master knowing that if the law could proof his presence at the scene of the crime the chances are the police and lawyers would make it look like he did it."

This drama made the judges to adjoin the case till 11:00 AM the following day and meanwhile requested and ordered that both Mrs. Wahkat and husband Abdulie Njie be remanded without any bail rights till tomorrow. The morning papers went wild and were full of the new state of affairs against fellow they dubbed the giant of crime, Mr. Crime Master/Rob.

As for Mrs. Wahkat Njie it seemed the day of judgement for her unsavoury life was about to bloom. The papers blamed Abdulie Njie for failing to let the law take its cause than way he went about disgracing his uncouth wife.

The development of this trial made many more to come and listen to it over microphones located at places in the compound. The trial would have been televised had there been one in the country at the time. The city was overflowing with visitors and folks eager to witness judicial history being made and also have opportunity to see the sky girl in the flesh and possible pose with her for memento of the visit.

Hence by 10:00 Am the next day of the trial the court room was full and guests waited in silence looking forward to the most dramatic unveiling of the day. At the hour of 11:00 Am the three judges in their red dress walked in and took their seats. The prisoner was brought under security escort as usual and placed in the cage as before.

Then two female prison guards walked in with Wahkat in chain between them. This was followed by Abdulie being brought in under heavy guard by police because he tried to kill himself last night. Will all of them seated, the judge asked Abdulie Njie be sworn and allowed to continue testimony he commenced the day before.

Abdulie, apologised but insisted his was not emanating from jealousy but purely not wanting to see an innocent man, no matter how vile he may be to others, to face the death penalty while he was innocent of the crime. He said, "I testify under the penalty of death that Crime Master had no hand in this ugly act but by an accidental act my wife, Mrs. Wahkat Njie hit the temple of Foday Faye to cause the fatal blow. I know my wife to be very brave lady and she would attests to my statement shortly. Aside what I said I know nothing about the why of it all." The completely overwhelmed prosecutor told the judges that he no further want to question any of the witnesses and that justice should take its cause.

However, the judges were not going to have matters rest at that. Judge Julia asked Abdulie, "What would have done had you earlier on caught your wife having an adulterous affair with male you assumed an honest reliable friend that you go fishing with on a weekly bases?"

Abdulie wasted no time. He told Judge Julia that love is blind and poisonous. He told her, "If the detractor happens to be one trusted most it was still wrong act and bridge of trust. Be a woman or man this was a very shocking thing that causes irrational acts. He definitely would have not killed Foday Faye but would beat the hell out of him before devoicing wife Wahkat Njie for good.

He would most likely castrate Abdulie Njie to render him a eunuch." Judge Julia thanked him and asked that he stepped down and wait by the escort guards. Then the drama all were waiting for unfolded as soon as Mrs. Wahkat Njie stepped onto the stand. The judge reminded her that she was still under oath and must now tell us the entire truth as it occurred 2:00 AM that night in question.

Mrs Wahkat broke down but later held her composure and facing the judges said, "All that my husband just narrated was true. He caught us making love and in the confusion I took the heave board to knock him out but he ducked making me hit

Foday Faye with full force of swing I gave it. I was wrong having an affair with men while being married to a faultless gentleman who had nothing wrong except his bad luck. He hardly makes a penny a day and I had to scratch for food, school fees and uniforms for the kids. With this overwhelming load of responsibility I fall victim to men ready to pay heavily for just a one night stand.

At first I could not stand having lowered my dignity but very soon got over it as the easy sweet money poured in daily. My husband had so much trust in me that he would walk away leaving me carry on as if nothing elicit was transpiring.

I even at one time hit him hard with a spoon and told him that he no longer loved me and that was why he cared very little about my disappearances and coming home very tired late at night. I will never have such a good man in my life again. I again testify that the fatal blow was accidentally caused by me and not Abdulie my husband.

I have nothing to add to this story other than I am sorry for death of Foday Faye and for being a bad wife to Abdulie Njie. Please exonerate him from any penalty in this case. It was all my mistake and doing because of lack of money." By the time she finished her last sentences tears were dripping like a broken fountain and running down her lovely cheeks leaving lines as they permeates thick make up she still had on.

One can notice figment of sympathy from the judges but they swore to uphold and carry out dictums of the law. The chief defence stood and said, "Your lordships the case has ironed itself out in the most miraculous and dramatic fashion.

None of us would have ever dreamt that such a beauty could be involved in so dangerous an action. The defence rest the case and demand complete exoneration and freeing of my client, Mr. Crime Master. It is up to court do what is required of you."

The judges decided to spend the night going over the case before advising the jury to vote on acquitting Mr. Crime Master and charging of the complicit couple. The jury and accused were advised to be at the dock at 9:00 Am the following day. Again the tabloids went crazy and some even suggested that Abdulie Njie be freed of all wrong doing for his wife did admit causing the fatal blow that ended Foday's life.

At the stipulated 9:00AM the judges filed to their seats and the chief judge started saying, "Throughout my judiciary experience with those of co judges we hardly come across a case so difficult and yet provided the necessary facts to enable us pass correct conclusions. For today the jury is advised to go into cession and weigh out only all the evident presented to this court.

The jury should reframe from personal emotions and innuendoes about the case. They should vote only according to their clear conscience and understanding of the case as presented in this court. You are now free to go to private room set for deliberation and to return a unanimous verdict of the case.

You can choose to vote on a second degree murder or first degree if that is what the majority saw fit in this case. We wish you the best of luck in your deliberation. We are available to advise any time your foreman calls or needs it to enable you precede your duty. Good luck." The next thing the judge ordered was removal of shackles from hands and ankles of Crime Master.

He told him, "The law finds you not guilty for the murder of Mr. Foday Faye which took place 2:00 AM at his home and we are sorry for hardship you experienced while in the arms of the law. You now are free to go about your business and try not to be involved in anything that would make society think of you as a misfit. Again, good luck."

On removing the shackles from his legs and hands Crime Master begged to address the court. He began saying, "Your lordships please accept my gratitude for your setting me free. I do want to plead for the two people now under custody of this court.

I beg that the court be lenient to both because it all happened because of very difficult circumstances Wahkat endured and above all seemingly innate bad luck that befell Mr. Abdulie Njie. Without honesty and brave gallant people like this couple I was definitely heading for the gallows as both tabloid and most of the public already stigmatized me as a master criminal. I am grateful to these two for being truthful instead of hiding behind lies for the rest of their earthly lives.

I did receive a call from Wahkat Njie who was my high school sweet heart but she left me when I travelled to Europe in search of greener pastures to get a better life than this reward less farming life. I see this case emanating from bazaar happening beyond the control of all involved.

I personally promise to turn into a new leaf and will clean up my life and work positively with society. Thank you very much for giving me lease of life and chance to be a good human being before I meet my maker. I have never and will never kill a fellow human."

A rapturous applause followed and lasted three minutes with even the judges and jury being moved by candour and desire to change from the region's most notorious felon. Police and security saluted him as he walked out of the court room with head held hide as if to tell his escorts to eat their hearts for there is a good in all. It only need be triggered to set alight.

Miss Binta Ceesay, Daughter

While at the door Mr. Crime Master told the news men to learn not to be bias about cases until they know all about root causes of it. He told the press, "I was certain that judgement was erroneously passed on because of stigmatization the media portrayed me.

From now on I will like to be called by my real name Amadou Sanne instead of the nickname so prevalent in your files on me. I was christened, Amadou Sanneh but the terrible name 'Crime Master' lingered and overshadowed my real name. In addition, I reassure all that I am from today a new man that would work for the good of the community and urge you not to be frightened in dealing with me.

I neither bite nor ever killed anyone. These vices were attached to me because some journalists drew comfort in maligning me and all I stood for." The statement busted the bubble and took the rug off the feet of the tabloids. None expected such sober thoughts from person they classed as an Ingrid lost in drugs, crime and pimping among many vices he was alleged to be involved in.

All is well that ends well. The jury took only six hours to reach its verdict on the case. Soon they file in court and took their seats and the foreman was summoned to face the judges and report on their decision. The fore man did exactly that and while in front of judges in a silent but parked court he read their agreed verdict. He said, "You lordships, we have unanimously reached a verdict as follows.

1. We all agreed and ruled that Mr. Crime Master, now in the cage not involved in this no matter his previous record.

2. We agreed that Abdulie Njie had intended to beat man he found having sex with his lawful wife. However the fact that he never carried the act but was honest about it we found him not guilty of any crime or assault to the victim Foday Faye nor did he caused his death.

3 The final verdict was the most difficult one because it kept us arguing for a while before we arrived at the following.

We unanimously found Mrs. Wahkat Njie to have accidentally killed Foday by inadvertently hitting him with a heavy board aimed at Abdulie Njie. We also want to please appeal for the court to exercise mercy when it renders its ruling. I really besieged your lordships to tamper justice with mercy in this case. With this we have done our duty as prescribed by law."

The Chief Judge thanked the Foreman and jury for a job well and then dismissed them home. He then ordered freeing of Abdulie Njie but Mrs. Wahkat Njie was to be detained until the passing of sentence in a weeks' time. Just as they were to go to their chambers Abdulie Njie came to centre of the court and pleaded to be heard. The judges sat and told him he has ten minutes to talk or go home.

Abdulie thanked them for the opportunity and said, "Your honour in your hands is life of my lovely wife. She never meant to do it. And I begged to be sentenced and hanged with her if that is judgement you are about to pass on her for an accidental crime. She has been bad but her intentions were made clear to this court and I forgive her for any wrong she did in this marriage because it was very difficult to sleep in unheated room and especially with only sugarless coffee and piece of biscuits to go with.

She has been good to me and our children and I rather die with her than let her take the blame alone. My bad luck had something to do with this outcome as explained to the court by my wife. Again, thanks a million for let me plead for my wife's life. God bless." This touching appeal left both judges and spectators moved.

A priest stepped forward and said, "Your lordships, verily, even God metres mercy to all who wronged him, especially if they are repentant. We certainly are taught powers of God for despite heinous nature of the act there is not a single soul here who is not seeking justice being tampered with mercy in this murder case.

All involved have spoken eloquently and truthfully beyond all expectations and we witness the change of an alleged supper criminal as portrayed by media because of candour of the ones now under custody presented their part in the tragic end of Foday Faye. In view of the above I also submit plea for mercy to be shown to lovely Mrs. Whakat Njie."

The news carried for two weeks varying aspects of the dream ending of the case. Some even ventured to say that Foday's ghost most have embed itself in these people to turn so caring to those that would have ended their lives at the gallows.

All eyes and ears were now trained at the judges who were to pass sentence at the end of a forth-night. People noticed that the space girl just grind or smiled when the last two people, Amadou Sanneh and Abdulie Njie took centre stage to plead their cases before the judges.

She seems to appreciate the effort than the wrangling between lawyers which was not only boring but looked sickening to her. It reminded her of record well before ten generation of her family, which put in human terms cover billions of years.

The two week came and passed quickly. On Monday of the judgement groups in large numbers urged the judges to be merciful and not to hang the poor woman who accidentally killed Foday Faye. Some reminded the judges of statement in the bible in which Jesus asked, "Let he who is sinless throw the first stone." None that were trying the prostitute in question ever did and with this being case the prisoner was set free.

The chief judge hit the gabble on the table to start the summery of the sentencing in the case. After long legal review of similar cases matched with gravity of this one the judge finally came to the natty-gritty that everyone wanted to hear.

Hence he said, "We have after long deliberation decided to award the defendant, Mrs. Wahkat Njie, mother of three children, a suspended sentence of second degree manslaughter. However, she will need to do three months of community service work and for another five years if during the said time she is known to be involved in assault or any act that may cause bodily harm she would summarily be subject to instant imprisonment for no less than fifteen consecutive years with hard labour.

At the same time anyone who decide to assault her because of constrain we placed on her that person or persons will be subject to trial and give long sentence for harassing Mrs. Wahkat Njie. The silent court room ruptured into ceaseless applause for good ten minutes before it died down.

The media being allowed to televise it nationwide had praises poured onto the three judges for being so kind and considerate. Even the family of Foday thanked the judges for being human and seeing it the way Foday Faye would have like her treated. Some rich merchant promised to help as well employ both she and husband Abdulie Njie as soon as she finishes her community work.

Only at this trial did our space girl failed to take centre stage of attention. The audience was too moved with what surprisingly unfolded before their own very eyes and life.

My 'Diriyanke/rose' Fatou Koma Ceesay, Manchester UK 2017

Chapter 7

RETURN TO SPACE

Hence after having brief meeting with the Justices the rain child was driven home to now prepare to take off to space and tell her earthly experience. As expected she invited Suntukung to visit after having had her own family and children. Suntukung Foro's parents gave a half hazard acceptance as they were not going to have their daughter to be the first human to climb to space to meet supper intelligent breeds.

A week later all Panyeki kunda, neighbouring villages and hamlets assembled at the Bantaba to bid the rain child farewell for a memorable visit to earth. At the bantaba, Suntuknug Foro said, "Once on a while something great happens for us. For me this friend from Love planet is the greatest gift my life would ever recon. I have learnt a lot from her and about love, truthfulness and commitment to community.

It goes without saying that I will miss her whole lot. Hence in your behalf allow me give her this carving as token of our friendship and desire for continued visit by her and her siblings along with any that would want to come to earth to help us love more." Then Suntukung Foro walked to her space friend and they kissed and hugged for quite a while before she could let go. Soon there was lightening and silver strike coming from the skies.

When the ladder settled the space girl took one step towards it and then addressed the crowd thus, "Humans, I had wonderful and very warm time with all of you. I found you very friendly and kind. Rest assured this will not be my last visit.

Again remember to be honest, caring and above all committed to each other. It will save you endless wars and social headaches you current endure. Thank you and good bye my friends". She ran to give last huge to Suntukung Foro before alighting on the silver ladder from above.

Soon people saw it disappear in a flash and the rain child was again reunited with her kind. Suntukung Foro became revered and some artists erected statures of the two girls at the last spot the silver ladder landed. People up to now know swore to the landing final take off of the rain child. They take tourist to where the statues are and to the spot and you would find mound supposed to be remains of the statues in commemoration of the visit at Famori kunda by the rain child.

Late that night people saw a bright light over room where Suntukung Foro sleeps. It was reported that her space friend brought her presence which would keep her young looking for a thousand years. Suntukung Foro did acknowledge the light and present but was not disclosing nature of it to the public.

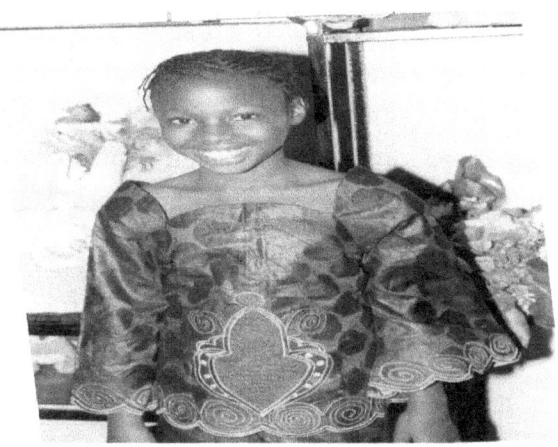

Miss Roheyata Ceesay, Daughter

Chapter 8

SUNTUKUNG'S LIFE THERE AFTER

Life after such phenomenal visit from space would never be the same again for young Suntukung Foro. All eyes and media were focused on her to envy of her peers. Girls literally seek her friendship and attention just to see themselves in journals or being interviewed about Suntukung by the media.

Despite gravid intention of the press to try and make an instant celebrity of Suntukung Foro she and her family resisted being one. Instead Suntukung Foro maintained a very serene life style and remained the simple farm girl she was before the arrival of the rain child.

With media calmed villagers started wondering why Sntukung Foro failed to take advantage of her gift in life and make a bonanza of fortune from it. And many months later and at a christening Suntukung Foro was made the master of ceremony just to pry out reason why she kept such low profile in life.

It was in the middling of the fanfare that one Griot stood up and praised Suntukung's linage for hours while at the same time receiving all sorts of gifts on behalf of Suntukung. Afterwards shy Suntukung stepped forward and thanked all present especially one that laid so much praises about her linage.

She said, "True the Foro linage is one I am proud of but we need move forward to curve poverty, illiteracy, healthcare, strive to get safe drinking water, good shelters and food to stop the current starvations in the region."

This said she sat and the press went frantic in trying to interview her or just finding out if she would like to throw her hat into the forth coming election for parliament. Suntukung Foro being aware of the power of the media had to quell such unfounded rumour before it becomes wild bush fire hard to put off without it having caused great damage.

Again she told the press at no time in her life would she contest for position in Parliament and that is the arena of politicians and not her. This was brushed down to her shyness. Some tried to create their own mythical political party of their own and at the same time naming her as its Secretary General.

She and her family refuted being part of such a myth or blessing such insults to their name and the Foro family threatened that legal action will be taken against the perpetrators should those responsible not place a retraction in the press and advertisements they already sent out.

Mean while Suntukung Foro, the teenage girl, is growing fast into a beautiful lady that the wealthy tycoons of the region started vying for. Again she kept her distance without being very aloof or abrasive to her many suitors. She loved Sambujang Kajali, who was at the time reading for his medical degree in France.

The only ones in the know were her immediate family and they were told never to fall for money over zealous wealthy men who might want to use money to buy her love or pay for her parent's greed. On one occasion a rich Mauritanian tried his luck for Suntukung by coming up with 100 camels, 100 bulls, 100 cows, 100 goats, 100 sheep and literally a hundred of anything he thought would convince the Foro family that he was the right man for their lovely Suntukung. Most women during Suntukung's days would feel themselves anointed if a wealthy man, as has occurred in numerous cases for Suntukung, offered them just two bulls for their hand in marriage. Hence many blamed Suntukung's parents for being foolish by refusing such a one time gift from the heavens.

The Foro family agreed that neither money nor material buys love. In marriage the two people involved must be in love and committed to each other for money can disappear in thin air leaving them and only true love can keep the union.

Kindia Koma Kunda: Bk L-R: Musa Koma, Jalian Ture, and Marota Koma. Front L-R: Mohamed Dembo Koma and Nice

Chapter 9

SUNTUKUNG FORO MARYS

Years passed before Sambujang Kajali returned home as a medical doctor ready to serve his people. He straight away set scouts to trace his high school love. At the same time friends told Suntukung of sighting a doctor recently returned from Europe who has remarkable resemblance to Sambujang Kajali but they have not establish his identity yet.

This sent sparks and tremors of excitement into Suntukung Foro. She could not wait to tell her mother who started worrying about Suntukung's constant refusal to accept previous suitors asking for her hand in marriage. Legend has it that on a clinic day at Janweli village the doctor saw a face that he dreamt of daily.

It had to be pretty Suntunkung that had sprouted to such a beautiful rose. So he walked toward the figure that was at the time chatting with a lady friend asking about the identity of the new doctor to sit in service that day. On turning the two strangers faced each other.

After a brief moment of doubt they both rush into each other's hands and kissed fervently for good five minutes before noticing attention they just sparked. The two walked quietly to the clinic amid admiring gazes from the crowd. The doctor asked his driver to take her to his bungalow while he sees the patients.

Before then, both she and Suntukung apologised the waiting crowd for display of their love for each other and delay they may have endured. He promised to see everyone even the late comer. At the bungalow Suntukung Foro pinched herself several times to make sure she was alive and not dreaming the coincidental discovery one she loves. She had finally retrieved her knight on a white horse ready to gallop with her to the bridal lane soon. She threw herself on the bed, got up went to the mirror and spoke to it as if it were human able to respond to the many questions she posed.

The excitement overwhelmed her and she fell asleep sprawl in the great doctor's king size bed. Dr. Sambujang Kajali hurried home after the last patient and on arrival parked the car as quietly as can be; walked to an empty seating room which made his blood curdle for fear that his dream girl could not wait and had returned home.

However just when he was about to dress and drive to her village he saw his lady lying in bed sound asleep. It was sight he had imagined many times while in France. Now it is happening for him in his own house and in his bedroom. He calmed down went to the kitchen and prepared the most delicious meals for them that evening.

Then he went and plugged the most beautiful rose from the garden and poured the most fragrant perfume on it. He then whiffs it twice across face of his future wife. The aroma woke Sutukung Foro and to her amazement her knight was standing right in front of her with bouquet of roses in hand for her.

Again they kissed and reminisced for an hour before heading down to have a bite at meal the doctor prepared. In the mean time Suntukungs parents started wondering because their daughter never stayed that late away. Should they set the alarm for scouts to search for her or should they wait a few more hours and see if she would turn up? Back at the bungalow the love birds hurried over their meal as it was getting late.

Suntukung and Dr. Kajali drove back to Panyeki kunda just in time to prevent the already organised search for Suntukung. Her mother leaped into the air in joy on seeing Suntukung and Dr. Kajali walking towards them holding hands. The great doctor said, "Both Suntukung and I apologised for this lateness in her return home.

We were like teenagers caught in trying to catch up elapsed time from our high school days to our surprised meeting at the clinic. I invited her to dine with me and hence the cause of her being late." Suntukung's parents were delighted to welcome Dr. Kajali to their humble home.

However it being late he promised to be with them at a more opportune time sooner than they expected. He having been in Europe for too long was not afraid of kissing Sunukung before gazing eyes of her parents. It made her mother smile and recalled her first kiss of Suntkung's father Mr. Foro some eons back.

As promised the doctor wasted no time to send his uncles to Suntukung's family asking for her hand in marriage. The two families had known each other through out time they existed hence it was just matter of formality to consecrate the two into matrimonial union.

Dr. Alhasan Ceesay graduating from the American University of
the Caribbean School of Medicine 1992

Chapter 10

SECRETE WEDDING PLANS

Some started contemplating what type of wedding this would be and where it would be held. Others were brave enough to believe it will be held in an Old French castle with only family and friends allowed to attend. Dr. Kajali and Suntukung kept their wedding plan as top secret.

For the Dr. Kajali wanted their wedding day and place not to be undisclosed until three weeks to the actual event. The family remained tight lipped and dignified than bloating about the luck of their daughter. This made the media nervous and anxious to gain control of the events as they unfold.

Hence they again, like in previous wealthy-do engagements, went into a frenzy of leaking half-truths and presenting interviews with retired teachers claiming to have taught the couple at various levels of schooling.

This was done to outwit and sell more than their competitors. The media even allowed speculation that the couple will be wedded in Paris or America instead of the Gambia. Thank God both the Medical Research College and Dr. Kajali band granting interviews to the media for fear of disruption of work.

Dr. Sabujang Kajali left for France to buy wedding presents for his bride and his entourage days ago and will not be back to PaFnyeki Kunda for three weeks. Suntukung Foro was very happy for gaining what she reported as, "A joy that will last till the end of time." The community sent presents and wished the couple a very successful and happy fruitful relationship.

They came to like the simple amiable person Suntukung Foro represented. Above all they respected Dr. Sambujang Kajali's honesty and for waiting as long as he did to marry his high school dream girl. Suntukung and her sister, Hadi, paid a quick visit to Dr. Kajali's surgery in Banjul to buy all the other wedding garments away from prying eyes and ears of media.

Sambujang Kajali's home was the epitome or zenith and trappings of wealth. He had few villas built in Senegal and districts in Gambia and even Sierra Leone of all places. Suntukung could hardly believe that that was going to be her empire and that all she had to do was to wish or ask and it shall be delivered on a golden platter.

On this visit they had their dinner on board one Sambujan Kajali uncles' luxury liners anchored at government wharf in Banjul. This ship was on the same day-renamed lady Suntukung's Paradise. All was set and blue-sky, moon and stars lit the way. The candle light dinner tables befit royalty and not for simple peasant girls like Suntukung and Hadi.

Dr. Kajali and the girls and invited friends ate with them and enjoyed music all the evening and then everyone retired to their luxurious cabins. The girls had arranged to sleep in the same cabin to keep promise of not being intimate with their future husbands until the day of their honeymoon.

Strange enough but this was how conservative and self-disciplined girls were during Suntukung Foro and Hadi's days. Yes, women jealously guarded their dignity until the right moment comes instead of falling for today's common one-night standers. The girls clandestinely left for Panyeki Kunda after being spoiled by lavish gifts by Dr. Sambujang Kajali and friends.

Chapter 11

DATE OF THE WEDDING SET

Media frenzy had now turned not only PaFnyeki Kunda but also the entire region into a state in painful gestation and expectant region's biggest event. Aching for the mother of all weddings everyone wondered where it would take place, whether the wedding was going to be private and who would be on the official invitation list of that historic day of days for the region. No one knew details of the wedding because the bride wanted to complete her preparation before letting the cat out of the bag.

Time has now allowed Suntukung to mature and grow beyond wildest expectations. She now acts maturely and is confident of herself. The plans were finally consummated at a family meeting held secretly in Banjul away from the Paparazzi and media. There the future couple agreed that the wedding would happen at the great hall of lovers in Panyeki Kunda the Gambia. The occasion will be an interfaith officiating and all major religions will be represented and will offer prayers.

It was agreed that the wedding take place on the first Friday after harvest to enable all villagers wanting to participate in the ceremony attend. A list of who is who not only in the Badibous but also in the political arena was wisely drawn from spectrum of politicians. The media started vying for locations and people to interview on the great day even though it would be three months before the girl takes her vows.

The tabloids and various village organizations went into frenzy of preparation as to who would be most artistic and perform the most remembered feat of all dances. Neighboring villages in Senegal cashed in and prepared to take the show on the day of days for the region.

Chapter 12

THE GRAND WEDDING

Panyekii Kunda is an old colonial trading center and gateway to the northern region of the Republic of Senegal. It lies on the grassy banks of the Miniminiyang bolong, a creek of the River Gambia, in the North Bank Region. Mandinka, Wolof, Fulas, Serere and a few Jolas inhabit Panyeki Kunda city.

In this fringes of the Gambia will soon take place the regions most historic even after the Saitmatie crusade in the 1920s. Both Suntukung Foro and Dr. Sambujang Kajali are members of the Mandinka tribe whose great grandparents migrated from now Republic of Mali to the Badibous in the Gambia.

Suntukung Foro was groomed, like her parents before her, to become a good farmer and housewife. Suntukung's great, great, grandparents, unlike the break homes these girls live in, lived in huts and mud houses some distance away from the fields.

Pnyeki was then a rural village with few thousand inhabitants with no roads, only bush paths through thick savanna grass. It had an abundance of cattle, horses, goats and sheep grazing in the vacant fields. Hence Panyeki Kunda has metamorphosis into the metropolitan city you are about to celebrate history of a magnificent twin wedding.

The momentousness of the occasion left Suntukung and Dr. Kajali at lost in the welter of thousand details. Every aspect was well orchestrated and their wedding dresses looked superb and admirable. Dr.Kajali and friends gladly paid for the bills and more.

All was set by midday of Thursday twenty fours to wedding day. It is reported that the rain child did visit Suntukung Foro to congratulate her on her wedding and left presents from her sky mates for her and Dr. Sambujang Kajali. Young ladies in towns and villages wished their day to be half as historic and romantic as the one they are about to witness.

They prayed that the rain child to notice them and rain good luck on their paths. Soon the Alice in wonderland wedding of prince and princess dawned. Mean while Panyeki Kunda swelled to almost quarter of a million by the last week of the month of the wedding. Buntings and flags flew all over the city as if it were going to have a coronation.

The Lovers hall at Hotel D'amour had a special facelift and a makeover with effigies of the ladies and their feature husbands on display. Security was beefed up well in advance of the ceremony for fear of trouble from competitors.

Friday, the day of the wedding, dawned bright and clear. Pnyeki Kunda was turned into the largest gathering of happy, cheering, smiling, dancing villagers, and onlookers lining the streets to have a glimpse of the cars of the brides and bridegrooms. Sea of People in celebrant mood struggled with flags, buntings in hand to see the bridal cars.

It was not until after midday that the procession to Hotel d'amour began with people cheering, throwing rice, flowers and even kisses at the bridal cars. The car crawled slowly because people eager and wanting to touch them or place their bouquet of flowers on them. Finally the bridal entourage reached the hall and proud and happy fathers of the lady met her at the door and walked the isles to hand Suntukung over to take their vows gracefully. Suntukung was just petrifying radiant and charming to behold. On this lovely Friday Suntukung Foro and Dr. Sambujang Kajali took their vows to be wedded husband and wife. This was good omen for villagers who just had a bumper harvest added to this once in a life ceremony in behalf of one their own.

The ceremony officiated by priests from all major denominations took full two hours before the married couples could stand at a special balcony erected for the purpose to thank those who in any way made it so warm and historic for them and Famori Kunda.

They then joined VIPs and invited guests at the banquet hall for the reception. From this formal reception the couples headed to the square at the center of the city, where the scene looked like a great sea of villagers, to witness the most colorful display of dance, acrobats, wrestling, and spectacular feat of magic performed by various groups and villages.

Yes, events of the wedding ceremony reverberated in every village and hamlet of the Badibous. The television, media and paparazzi had a field day and many people vied to be interviewed or photographed while hold pictures of the wedded. Dr. Kajali and friends jointly provide all the food, a dozen bulls were slaughter for the villagers to feat on.

The celebrations continued to the wee hours of the night before the people went to rest. It picked from where it ended on Friday right through Wednesday before the celebrants called it quit. Famori was overwhelmed with the sense of history and joy this wedding brought to it.

The city will never be the same again for it will now be inundated with more tourists than it ever dreamt of. Mean while the married couple had left quietly to one of Dr. Kajali's villas to spend their honeymoon. On the night of the honeymoon the two were lost in the whirlwind tide of need and longing.

They were immersed in the sea of old memories and sensations. Suntukung slid her hands up his back, brought him closer and heard him groaning against her mouth as he deepened the kiss while threading his fingers through her hair. She could not believe that she has the joy of her life right then that will last her till the end of time.

 Dr. Kajali in ecstasy and ragged breathing said, "I have dreamt about doing this for a long, long time. I wanted it, longed for it and now we are here in each others' arms and it is right, so right." It felt right to both as he smothered her face and neck with endless kisses. He slid his hands under her bra making her feel the heat of his fingers causing her to arch against him feeling her nipples harden instantly.

She loved it and when drawn closer to him, she felt his heart beating rapidly against hers.' She instantly felt a pleasurable heat beginning to spread deep and low in her stomach. Suntukung savored every moment of the experience and in being in her mans' arms ready to make love to her for the first time since they met during their high school days.

They returned two months later with Suntukung Foro pregnant. With ceremonies over, it was time for the couple to head back to answer requests from their French friends wanting to serenade their union.

They took off from Yundum International this time hand in hand amid cheers and well wishes from friends and family who came to see them off to France.

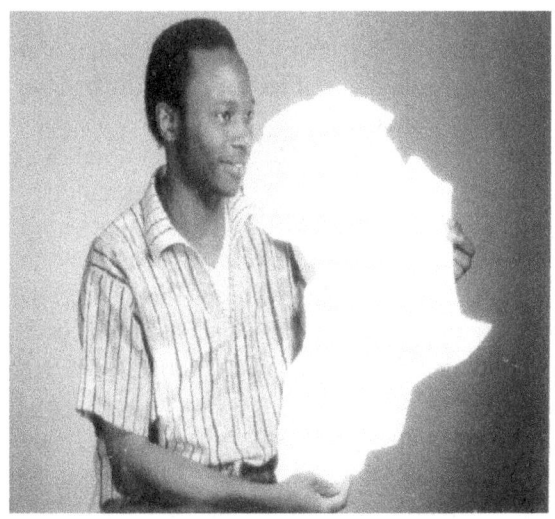

Dr. Alhasan Ceesay holding Africa

Chapter 13

THEIR DAY IN FRANCE

Friends and residents at Paris were not ready to be left out in celebrant mood for now Dr. Kajali was a popular student whose marriage need be recognized in fashion by friends.

Newspapers and the paparazzi were at Charles Deguals International Airport waiting for flight GA737 to touch down so as to get first hand scoop and pictures to sell.

Journalist from all over the West Africa swarmed the terminal to have photos and write on the emerging couple. Why?

It is unusual for such educated youngsters to be wood by love and not wealth. The couple stole the limelight at both ends. It was historic wedding as educated African wives being much more in the limelight than their husband tend to run the show instead which renders some men impotent.

Hence, in most of such marriages, instead of reconciliation, the males end up dumping their educated wives and taking on obedient uneducated village girls. For Dr. Sambujang Kajali to woo Suntukung Foro their return to France was like an Alice in Wonderland romantic tale plus the dignitaries that graced the occasion all added an enigma to the whole scenario and events that took place at Famori Kunda in the Gambia, West Africa.

Paris being city which the couple would frequent geared up to show France's hospitality and generosity.

The minister for Health and the Lord Mayor of Paris both got in touch with the President and soon it was announced that one of the Ministers would grace the civic ceremony planned for recognition of the couple's promoting of West African Francophone fraternity and cultural understanding abroad.

There was a contingent of palace dancers and the President's son, at the Charles Degual's International Airport to welcome the couple back to France.

The magical performance of the dancers amazed all present and the match pass was full of pump and brings to memory and attention of African history and regal epics.

The band plaid one of their ancient tunes slow match music as soon as Dr. Kajali and, now Mrs. Sutukung Kajali, emerged from the plane. Next to alight were Dr. Kajli's best maid and entourage. Each received a bouquet of roses from the president's son in attendance after a warm handshake and saying, "Welcome back to France your second home away from home."

The paparazzi were kept at bay but that was just to allow the prince to do his thing before hell broke loose. Photographers elbowed, forth and pushed their way to get a chance to take snapshot of the newlywed, shall we say the newly re-wedded. An hour later Journals show headlines and pictures of the arrival ceremony at Degual's International airport.

The papers sold like mad raising millions for the industry.

Off they went to a secret location, chosen by France, to allow the couple reorient themselves back to real life. This would never be the case for both the media and paparazzi have tasted blood and want more and more of it.

The profit soared to 17% higher than sales of the same period in the entire period of last year. There was much surprise to come for the couple as both Prime Minister and Lord Mayor have agreed that the President Grace the dinner banquet scheduled for the returning newlywed. Saturday evening was the gala-day and big thank you show to recognize the couples' contribution to Ghanaian trade and cultural exchange.

The first thing that signaled that a big thing was afoot was the presence of plain and uniform security all over the hall and the fact that the PM and Opposition leader were already at the front row when the couples were ushered in by presidential guards. When all were seated the President entered through a well-guarded door took his seat after the national anthem.

The decorum was marvelous and the first lady radiant in her traditional Ashanti dress chosen for the occasion. To the delight and amazement of all it was the first lady who gave a short welcoming speech to the bride and bridegroom.

Then the president, who took opportunity to show his party cares about France and all of Africa, was followed by the Lord Mayor of Paris and then The PM, who also not only welcomed them home but also told how his party cares about citizens of France and Africa. The opposition leader gave slightly long rambling politically loaded polished speech before taking his seat. Dr. Sambujang Kajali gave response to the speeches.

He unlike the Prime Minister did not beat about the bush when he said, "Mr. President, Madam First lady, PM, all gathered here, we are honored and humbled by this magnificent recognition of our simple daily human acts. We thank the president and people of France, bowing towards the president, "for kindly gracing our day.

It is a pleasure to note that the French government does appreciate civil input and lives we touch. Thank you all for celebrating with us." He raised a glass and asked all to toast to France and the president and wish them long life and happiness. He took his seat and everyone including the President filled up on all sorts of dishes from Africa, the Caribbean and off course the Gambia and mostly a majority from French cuisines.

It was a momentous feast that the couple never dreamt would happen for them in their lives. The next surprise of the evening was the PM announcing that the couples report to the Palace a week after to receive France's colors and medals in recognition of their good contribution to Afro-Franco solidarity in the region. What else could happen for these that just united their lives?

So it its true to err is human but to forgive is indeed divine. Here we witness the rise of people who never met for nearly twelve years before love glued them and gave joy that will last till the end of time.

They became instant celebrity and even served as goodwill Ambassadors for France, Gambia, and the United Nations while back in the Gambia politicians vie to have them grace their party podiums. Three years later the couple decided to move permanently to the Gambia their homeland. They named their first baby boy after the first president of Gambia, in honor of his effort for the country.

Normally tradition has it that the firstborn boy be named either after the bride's father or grandfather and the first girl after the bridegroom's mother or grandmother. However, Suntukung Foro and Dr. Sambujang Kajali agreed that the only way to reciprocate was to name their first boy after the greatest president Gambia and Africa ever had.

Nonetheless by the end of the year some papers had definite sighting of the couple even though they were not able to interview them. To the very day Sutukung tries to remain anonymous and do enjoying reading stories made about them and their fairy tale marriage.

Musu Kebba Saidy in pink with a friend, Bakau Pipeline, 2017

Chapter 14

ODES TO TENDER LOVING CARE: TLC

This Ode is dedicated to those who tirelessly gave themselves for the love of the other. A hungry peasant in the street given a piece of bread, a penny or a shilling makes his day and only caring love made the giver act in kind.

Yes, the little acts of kindness we show are lives saving and it helps to give hope to others, especially the despondent and down trodden. Ignorance can at times be callous as demonstrated in the treatment of lepers in the olden days.

Today a bit of TLC and medication allowed these to leave among society instead of spending the rest of their earthly life in dark caves and doomed dungeons. Carriers of the aged, the sickly and disable deserve mention in being among the greatest golden hearts of our time. Bravo to all those gallant men and women who go to help in disaster zones, earth quakes, fire, or other catastrophes.

They do this out of love for you and me at the risk of their own very lives. I applaud wholeheartedly farmers who keep our breadbaskets filled, sailors who brave turbulent stormy oceans to get commerce moving, fishermen who challenge fires and angry seas to land a catch in other to provide us delicious fish meals, teachers who impart knowledge in us and all those bright minds that fly the metal bird to make global trotting lot easier than Christopher Colombo's days.

There is no greater TLC than it. Those with Alzheimer suffers can for sure attest to the dedication, patients, and love these unique people show as being fact of pure love for the self and others. No one can pay enough for the services of the housewife with husband and ten kids running around, Nurses, doctors, teachers, corers, police and even the solder.

What they give to society keeps all safe and informed for the day. They give safe TLC to allow us have restful nights like babies in slumber land and wake up to more TLC. Even young women can at times be overheard telling their friends that they intend to give tender loving care to their men when the men return from work. Yes, everyone needs and love TLC ala cart. Do not we feel great in the loving arms of our wives or lovers or mums?

One should be thankful when someone else cares about us. Note the love and care a mother gives to her newly born. Nothing is greater TLC than maternal love and the eventual bonding that ensues between mother and child. Love makes us forgive and forget pain inflicted on us. Without TLC the world will be in endless storms.

TLC is a charitable act that pervades all spheres of communities. TLC makes our hearts etched in others forever. TLC gives inspiration to the despondent and down trodden and it raises our spirits to higher heights. Hurray To TLC! Cheers to my wife, and friends for loving me and for caring for both of us in this life.

Tender loving care is phenomenon found in all higher mammals. Just watch documentaries about our cousins' monkeys, Apes, Gorillas, and Chimps and one would certainly note tender loving care being endlessly dispensed.

In the ghetto Tender Loving Care implies giving heart, soul, and feeling to the self and others. TLC magically transience gender and age. The old lady or man afraid of crossing the street would tell you relief he or she had from the gentle touch of a Scout or a police officer volunteering to help them cross to the other end of the street. It was all TLC in action and it leaves gratifying feeling for both giver and receiver.

"Always be my TLC." A true friend once sent this wish to me on my 50th birthday being a valentine day while I was in America. Hence we valentines do receive lot of cheers and TLC on our revered February 14th day of our lives.

It is normally said that business neither has a heart nor does it bleed but take it from me it does give TLC to its shareholders and governments that can dole millions if not billions of taxpayer's money to bail them for eating or spending in unsafe investments our invested monies within their worldwide network of banks.

TLC is strong feeling almost mystical in itself. I wish governments had the same heart or TLC to bail out ordinary folks like you and I from grips of unyielding joblessness, poverty and disease. Aids, Malaria, AK47dictocrats of the developing world, and rampant corruption are drowning mankind. Where has the governments' TLC for man gone? We asked.

TLC, TLC! My brothers and sisters bind us for good. At times I hear people moaning about the emptiness of life and turbulent waters it landed them. The urge to tell or ask if they ever tried the not so much of panacea TLC for it could just be the bridge they needed to get them over trouble waters of their lives.

Tender loving care to you and may TLC forever remain etched in our hearts. TLC is bounty wider than the Atlantic and deeper than any earthly ocean. The more we give ourselves to help others the more we receive from it. Like my valentine card, back in my student days in America yearned, I too ask readers to always give tender loving care to themselves and others. Cheers.

Cherished Cousin Yamarie Sey, Faji Kunda, Gambia 2016

Chapter 15
A VILLAGE ALKALO (MAYOR)

With both Dr. Kajali and Suntukung Foro back home the city of
Panyeki Kunda elected Suntukung Foro-Kajali to be its first
female mayor in recorded times. Her popularity, domino and
relation with the rain child all helped to propel her into
leadership. Her leadership was omen of good luck for Panyeki
Kunda. Her tenure as village head was so productive that other
village heads come to her seeking advice.

There were no crimes committed or any discord among residents
and above all the village enjoyed bumper harvests throughout her
time.Residents named a few streets in honor of Suntukung's good
guidance and peace experienced by the people of Panyeki Kunda.
The only case ever brought before her concerned the case of
Fatima Sawaneh's forced marriage to one Keluntang Camara of
Nfamori kunda village.

The story has it that since birth of Fatima her father had literally
sold her for dowry of two cows and fifty gold nuggets from the
family of Keluntang Camara. Witnesses attest to the fact that both
the Camara clan and those of Sawaneh did agree on the said deal
when Fatima was in her mother's belly.

Wudeh Jaite, Fatima's mother, forth against premature marrying
of her unborn daughter out of greed instead of love. She had
support of her family but being married to the Sawaneh clan they
no longer had veto power to overrule wishes of their in-laws.

It so happened that in those days' women had little to say on who
their daughters or sons wed. It was the fathers and uncles who
make such pivotal decision for the children.

Wude Jaite and her daughter Fatima were ready to bell the cat or
call it to be the first rudiments of African women liberation
movement. It was Keluntang Camara who angrily brought the
case before Mrs. Suntukung, village head of Panyeki. She at first
tried to dampen the affair by requesting that the two families try
to settle the argument with the arbitration of village elders.

Wude Jaite having heard about Keluntang's chauvinistic attempt decided that the case should be heard in the open for all to pass binding judgment on it. The Camara clan, due to change of plans, insisted that instead of being given Fatima as daughter in-law they now want dowry they paid eighteen years back before Fatima was born.

Hence this started causing rift in the village which let village head Suntukung to summon the elders and council and set up a hearing date to settle the affair before it lead to nastiness between two friends. It was agreed that the case be heard after Friday prayers when nearly every respectable person would be present in the village instead of the farms.

This being test case for female village head, Suntukung Foro it drew quite a bit of attention causing lot more villagers from as far as Sabuyo to attend the case in judgment of ability of the only female village head there ever been in history.

The tabuloo was struck to call all concern to attend the hearing. Soon the Bantaba was jam packed with curious folks vying to know how Suntukung would dispense justice that would be unshakable. With all seated in dead silence the chief Griot got up chanted few historical praises about the Foro clan, Suntukung's clan and sat down to allow the priest offer prayer for the deliberation to go on smoothly.

This done, village head Suntukung cleared her throat and said, "Fellow citizens, we are assembled under sad circumstances for marriage connote joy, love and peace not the serious wrangle we are about to hear from contenders. The case regard dowry the Camara clan paid to Hadume Sawaneh father of Fatima Sawaneh lady now contested for by the Camara family.

I do request cooperation from each and everyone to make this as solvable as possible for the rivaling parties. I now call upon Karajang Camara to tell us why the u-turn in the whole affair of historic ties between to the families before us." Mr. Karajang Camara, being almost six feet nine inchies tall looked bending when he walked to the centre of the Bantaba ring and raised his hand and swore that all what he will tell will be nothing but the truth and that he trust the bitter truth will prevail in the case they are about to hear. He began, "It was during the rainy season of eighteen years back that my friend Hadume and I made the usual gentleman's agreement that should he ever have a baby girl he would let my boy Keluntang Camara, who was then seven years old, to marry his daughter.

He let me know that he would discuss it with his family and relatives and get to me as soon as possible. It would a week before he sent Almami Kinte to let me know the Sawaneh clan would like me meet with then on Friday evening of that week. I agreed and told my own team to accompany me to the august meeting.

Such clan meetings are recorded by Griots for the benefits of the children and future generation of the tribes. We met at the stipulated time and place. I have Argfan Sambu Koli, Mamadi Suware and Fanta Camara to support my statement as they formed team that went me.

After the normal cordialities it took only an hour to arrived at the agreed dowry of two bulls and fifty nuggets of pure gold for the hand of his then unborn daughter. I there and then gave the fifty gold nuggets to Arfang Sambu Kolli who after counting them to make sure it was fifty nuggets and not less handed the said gold nuggets to grinning Hadume Sawane.

He too counted and agreed that it was indeed fifty gold nuggets required by him as part dowry payment for hand of his daughter in marriage. He being satisfied told us thus, "Thank you for extending historic ties that had been since the existence of the two clans.

You can bring the two bulls between now and six months and I guarantee that even if this one did not survive the next girl to follow will still be your son's wife." Despite Wude Jaite's protest about the arrangement she received no heeding from anyone in attendance.

This said and done we prayed and dispersed. However three months ago we sent a decoy to find out Mr. Hadume Sawaneh's under current activities concerning one tycoon said to pay him five times the gold I already paid down as dowry and that he, Mr. Hadume Sawaneh had several discussion about it with his daughter and her mother. It was revealed that Wude Jaite swore to commit suicide if the tycoon was not given Fatima her daughter in marriage. On proving the story to be true I sent Arfang Sambujang Kolli back to the Sawanehs and requested gold and two bulls I paid as dowry for Fatima.

Mr. Kolli was told to mind his business and that if I have any doubts to confront the Sawanehs and not send emissaries to them about their daughter's future. I got very angry and disappointed to cause me meet Hadume at his farm and at first told him off before requesting he return all that was due me in three weeks time or I would take necessary steps to recoup my property from him. He now had two days left when I was summoned to appear before my peers to settle the case.

It is very difficult to have to speak in public about families that stood for each other millions years back. I thank all present and I have nothing to add to this ugly situation other than that I want my fifty nuggets of pure gold and two bulls back by Monday."

Suntukung thanked him and then told the gathering you are to familiarize yourself to the other side of the coin as Mr. Hadume Sawaneh is now called to stand to be judged by his peers.

Gentleman Sawaneh walked gallantly and stood like a warrior before the already angry crowd about to lynch him should he be dishonest or reneged on an agreement he made some eighteen years ago regarding his daughter future husband.

He started his story by greeting the village head, council elders and all present. Then he said, "I too stand before you seeking judgment for my actions regarding previously arranged marriage between my daughter Fatima and Keluntan Camara son of Karajan Camara.

Yes, Karajang and people he just named did approach me for the hand of my daughter Fatima Sawaneh in marriage and after ironing out details of the dowry I acquiesced to their request.

An advance payment of fifty pure gold nuggets was made and later two bulls were added meeting all that was required for the affair to be implemented. Its right and proper to point out at this juncture or time that my wife Wude Jaite mother of Fatima did protested against the deal because she felt one cannot buy or sell true love and that she rather we waited until the child was born and matured to be part of such earth shaking decision making about its life. All of us laughed and shunned her point. Then five month ago Mamadi Suware secretly calls my attention to fact that the Camaras have engaged pretty daughter of Sambu Fatie two days walk from here.

I asked Karajang Camara to meet with me about it but he turn down my request on several occasions, one of which was in presence of Malifi Njie seated before. Hence when he showed up at the farm I thought he at last have seen it fit to come to terms with reality. I had no problem of him changing his mind about our arrangement for that is human.

However to my surprise he gave me an ultimatum to pay up or face the full wraiths of the law. We had hot argument to cause other farmers like Junking and Musa to come to pour cold water over the debate. He walked away threatening to sue me if by mid day coming Monday I fail to deliver his entire dowry package back.

I discussed it with my wife who then told me that Fatima was indeed being wood by one tycoon not far from home. I told her that would be against the rule of civility but because Karajang had changed his mind about his son marrying Fatima we most try all reasonable means to get the gold for him before he disgraces me in court or before my peers.

I personally called Fatima and asked if she was indeed wood by the tycoon and was he her love. She emphatically told me she would kill herself if I submit her to Keluntang whose father stood to disgrace the Sawaneh clan. It was then that my wife and I went to the tycoon and sounded him out about the affair.

Here is what he said to me that day, by the way he is seated next to chief council man Fatajo in the gathering, "I love your daughter and could have eloped with her, as suggested by her, but I told her my love was too true to do any think like that. It was then that we agreed to approach her family.

It was then tearful Fatima told me that her father sold her to the Camara clan who later changed their plans and had married another girl two days walking distance from Panyeki."

He immediately offered three hundred and fifty nuggets of gold free to me and my wife. I now want the court to count these fifty nuggets of pure gold and pass it onto Karajan Camara. Also I would like the village head to kindly accompany me to my herd for us to select two bulls to be given to Camara."

There was a hush noise but everyone turn to the village head Suntukung to see how she would relate the case. She conferred with few close elders by her side and then said, "Unless Karajang denies statement made by Hadume, we would now ask scum bat Mamadi Suware to testify all he did in this fray."

Mamadi Suware did not like being tarnished by a woman more so in the presence of his fellow men. So he angrily stood at the centre in very chauvinistic attitude and began his testimony saying, "It look like a dark cloud is about to descend on men. We now have girls telling us what to say."

Suntuikung cut him off and threaten to jail him right away should he make the next rude utterance towards women. This timely intervention made the crowd cheer and ask permission to lynch one they now saw to be root cause of the trouble between the Cararas and Sawaneh clans.

Mamadi apologized and continued thus, "I felt disappointed that Karajang would renege on a gentleman's agreement accepted as part of our culture and tradition." This clarification calmed things down for the crowd now agrees with him on point he just made. One elderly urged, "Continue your briefing because the emotional ones want to finish you but you might be right in your actions. What happened next?"

Mamadi smiled and told how he arranged to disclosed all he knew that Karajang did and how he planned to recoup his gold and animals should Hadume fail to meet his deadline by coming Monday.

Only Keluntang, who is deadly in love with Fatima jumped the fence and threatened the Sawanehs despite fact that his father has gotten another bride for him without telling Keluntang. This made the crowd very angry about Karajang's uncouth behaviors. He finished by apologizing to all women especially one presiding over the case.

He said, "Madam Suntukung, please note that I never meant to say what nastiness I said about women. You are our mothers, sisters, lovers, and indeed trusted life time friends in this life. And I reiterate full respect for the female gender." This made ladies smiled and pleased with him at the same time saved his neck.

He sat down and next to testify was none other than Keluntang camara. He insisted he be give chance to exonerate his childish acts towards the Sawanehs. He said, "It never occurred to me that my father would be this twisted. Marriage is serious affair and link between two and cannot be flump flopped.

I never knew of my new bride until this case. I ask why I was kept in the dark about my own future. Time has made me love Fatima but it was lately that I found out she in reality never had an iota of attachment for me.

I tried to tell Fatima's dad but my father thought he could kill two rabbits with one short. He has now made me lose on both sides of the isles for the others will from now on definitely have nothing to do with him. They will deem him unworthy of being a father in law to their daughter and I most definitely do not like the new girl he got out of the blue.

Young Fatima and I agree that we are not for sale and that we want to be free to select our life partners and not through current ancient system that does not recognize women nor care effect their so-called historical friendly ties affects the future of those linked in this bond.

I therefore at this Bantaba of the elders sincerely apologies to the Sawaneh clan and especially ask for forgiveness to Fatima Sawaneh who has become the innocent victim of the affair."

This was followed by even a greater surprise testimony coming from none other than Fatima Sawaneh who begged to reciprocate Keluntang's candor.

The elders and Suntukung conferred and soon Fatima Sawaneh curtseyed and began thus, "Elders and comrades we have thus heard how parents weave life of their progenies into blinding life. I was not aware of my being literally bonded to Keluntang until on my seventeenth year, by the way I am nineteen now, because father thought fifty gold nuggets and two bulls was all I worth for him. I am human and not for sale father. Besides women too are endowed with brain and do use it better at most times than men." This comment drew groans from men and loud counter cheers from women. An old woman walked to her, kiss and danced around her in mark of traditional appreciation for Fatima's forthrightness.

Now the excited crowd shimmered to allow Fatima to continue thus, "Further more I would like to tell the tycoon to collect all he ever gave my parents for our discussions were purely my way of teaching dad a civics lesson so that he would not sell the next baby girl of his life. I declare that Keluntang and I be given chance to sail our own boats and cross tempest that may be our fate and not be forced into painful cohabitation."

This said Keluntang Camara transfixed by power and passion of love rushed to the centre of the Bantaba where Fatima Sawaneh stood. He knelt and in tears asked Fatima to marry him.

He before she could stop wiping her own tears, placed a 2000 karat gold ring into her finger and looked straight to her face and said, "The world and all love Goddesses awaits your reply. Without you I have no one to share this life with."

Fatima knelt and raised her hands to the heavens with tears of joy dripping off her lovely cheeks replied, "I too love you and will sail this life with you for better or worst side by side shall we endure the joys and hillocks of life." Then the two looked straight where their parents located in the thick of the crowd and said, "This is the correct way.

We will work to pay Karajang Camara gold nuggets Hahume Sawaneh took on our behalf from him." The crowd was stunned by this twist in the case and way these children surfaced. Stunned village head and sage Suntukung Foro then stood and said, "Fellow residents a few points must be cleared.

There is nothing wrong with tradition but it must reflect the times. It is time for us to have an open mind about life as it presents itself today.

Traditionalist thought overindulgence with current trendy life led pretty Fatima Sawaneh to become a wild nymphomania or is shockingly disregarding tradition and shaming the name of the Sawaneh clan.

These kids demonstrated to us in daylight that greed always ends in misery and this case exemplified that for both Karajang and Hadume. It is clear that Karajang would walk over his granny for recognition and wealth.

The kids did continue historical ties of the two clans but not in the exchange of goods in fashion the old tended to do things. Let us allow them live their dream in peace. The kids have showed us charming way to marriage.

I hope parents will from now on wait at least until their child reach adulthood before suggesting some unknown for them to spend the rest of their lives with. Fatima's experience reminded me of my teenage days when filthy rich men poured in gifts for my hand in marriage to which I refused and had their monies returned immediately.

I hence hope that no parent would be tempted to sell their children. This one sidedness must stop as we never see boys being traded the way girls are sold. I now declare the Bantaba meeting closed"

This speech angered a few elderly men but most agree that it was time to be inclusive and allow their ladies a say in the affair of the family especially on important matters such marrying the kids. The village head, amidst applause walked to Keluntang and Fatima and congratulated them for being honest with their feeling for each other.

Chapter 16

ALL IS WELL THAT ENDS WELL

Now that Keluntang and Fatima had declared their love for each other tradition and culture took over. Deep down we all love and want to be loved, and marriage was one successful sanction society we lived in embraced.

Liberated or not, be fully aware that there is no Miss perfect or mister right knight with shining armor ready to sweep us off our feet to the bridal lane.

Everything in life conforms to laws or else grave suicidal end results such as drugs, crime, prostitution and high alcohol binging or consumption would follow our intransigency. In Africa marrying into a family makes one a full member of that family and all it extended tentacles.

Keluntang is now duty bound to send his representation from the Camara clan, which has to include his father and uncle, to formally seek hand of Miss Fatima Sawaneh in marriage.

An intra family reconciliation took place before the delegation headed for Panyeki to iron out the new dowry. Hadume Sawaneh, Fatima's father, insisted on a much lower amount of ten gold nuggets of 100 karat value plus three cows instead of two bulls to be added as final package.

The Camara clan met the required dowry within two weeks and the wedding was set to take place three weeks thereafter at the grand mosque in Famori village where the Camara clan leaved.Very soon village after village sent in their contributions and some made special embroidery for the bride to wear. Panyeki village head; Suntukung Foro donated ten goats, four bulls and hundred bags of rice plus two barrels of fresh palm oil for use by the visitors.

This further earned her support and love of the villagers. Undoubtedly villagers poured into Famori Kunda to visit and witness marriage of Keluntang Camara and Fatima Sawaneh on the designated Friday. The moment the priest finished consecrating the union dancing and singing filled the air and everyone was more than happy for the newly wed.

Tribes from the region and afar poured in not only to participate but also to show their gratitude to the couple and also witness another unique occasion for the region. It was rare thing for elders to be challenged the way Keluntang did but it was the dawn of a new era that must be accepted by all.

Fatima and Keluntang are to have their historic moment celebrated in way they choose. So everyone was elated and danced to their heart's content in marking the true meaning of the day for the couple and celebrants. It was a cheerful and memorable day that none of them would ever forget.

The drums, dancing, chanting of scribes was spectacular. The bride and bridegroom were overwhelmed with bundles upon bundles of presents and animals lined up for slaughter in their behalf. At the banquet mayors and village heads of the region gave long speeches as what an exemplary thing these couple had been to them all. People praised them over and over and wished them happiness in their lives together.

It was a joyous occasion for all Suntukung concluded. The region's representative follows with similar line of comments and again prayed for the pair's happiness. The mayor of Njawara spoke in behalf of the villagers and pointed out the impact their example had on civic life of the villagers. **He was personally indebted to them eternally and would name his next child after Fatima if a girl and Keluntang if it turns out to be a male. Everyone laughed but understood the significant of it. It was an honour bestrode a few for such a remarkable Mayor to name one of his after an individual.**

The ceremony went on until late at night before the celebrants retired to bed. It being a marriage that signaled a new way the youths asked that they are allowed to bring a band from Mali to serenade Sunday following the traditional wedding ceremony.

Arrival of the Mali band to Famori kunda coincided with one from Senegal. The two modern music bands played right through the wee hours of Tuesday before the festivity stopped. The next day the couple flew to Banjul for a two weeks tourism or visit.

They returned to their jobs two weeks late but with Fatima carrying triplets for Keluntang. She refused maternity leave until two weeks to her due day before taking rest to prepare for the arrival of the babies.

Legend has it that the couple spent their honeymoon in Bathurst, the capital of colonial Gambia. And are now proud parents of five children who had as of today given then lovely grandchildren to propagate their genes.

This story would do disservice if it fails to remind readers to note that historic female village head, Suntukung, despite being favored by the rain child from space, never for once showed pomposity and had always served her people to the best of her ability.

However this work would be incomplete if it did not end with similar miracle story about petrifying Bere Kolong queen of love who leaved next to Dobo Forest in the Lower Badibou District of the North Bank Division of Gambia.

Ismaila Ceesay, Njawara, badibou, NBR Gambia 2016

Chapter 17

THE MYSTRY BERE KOLONG QUEEN OF LOVE

At a region called Bere Kolong near chakunda in the Badibous dwelled the most beautiful female figurine that only a few unfortunate young men chance to encounter. She is said to be parched amidst panorama of roses the like of which is found nowhere on earth.

Calamitous indeed for this sweetheart of the spirit chouses her lover and wards off any female that would dare flirt for her chosen mate.Her name was Jina Nyima, Alias Bere Kolong Masibo or the invisible spirit of love in the local vernacular. By the way Bere Kolong means stone well.

Jina Nyima was so tantalizing that any man other than the one she selected, gazing upon her is immediately turned into a stone at the position he stood. Hence up to today there stood many tall stones in the shape of men near Bere Kolong.

Her method of recruiting a lover starts as early as when the male child was born. It is said that through her supernatural powers she would make her new male partner grow faster than most children, bigger, taller and normally a lot stronger than any of his peers. She infuses these traits to send signal to other humanoid females who might set eyes and hearts on her would be lover.

Jina Musa was Jina nyima's father and he regretted his daughter being in love with humanoids instead of Jini like her. Because of this irreconcilable state between them he cast a curse upon her and varnished to Jina Dou and never returns to Bere Kolong.

Jina Nyima lived in a huge cave near the milky well whose waters served her. Only this milk like water quenches her thirst any other would leave her dehydrated and unable to function. It was reported that only one soothsayer or chief village Witchdoctor at a nearby village knew that the water from this particular source was her life being cursed by her father Jina Musa.

To secure her life she cast a guarding-spirit around the well making humans coming ten meters to it go blind instantly. Any who ventures beyond the ten-meter boundary are turned into stone, hence the name Bere Kolong in the local lingo.

It sounded crewel that such a beauty would guard its jewel fiercely and so close to its heart. This no man's zone or periphery enables her to walk free and live free with the man of her heart. In this way, she literally steals her mate and keeps him kidnapped at the cave while feeding him the best kingly feasts and drinks from the heavenly milky waters of Bere Kolong.

In the event of any girl getting astray to the well to fetch water she is normally not turned into stone but her mind is cryptically controlled and she ends up being a servant at the cave.

Should this servant chose to have any feeling for her mate both are instantly blinded and turned into weeds to be fed upon by grazing animals. Jina Nyima is said to have many half-man and halftime mutants roaming about, especially at night.

Villages claim to hear them singing and dancing or just playing magic to entertain themselves. The natives even believe that men with extreme physique amongst them may be her children she planted in the region.

Friday nights were nights the villagers for fear of angering the jubilant jinni kid accepted these nights as self-imposed curfew nights. The young jinni kids' playground was on top of mountain Kuku Konko near Bao bolong creek.

Atop of this mountain balls of fire work fill the night skies to the periled of any venturing to the sight. If any is seen by the mutant one is normally surrounded by a powerful cyclone and swept to the cave to serve as slaves doing the chores for the queen jinni and her mate.

The Mystery Jinni requires no food or eats anything but do need the milky water to enable a human male to inseminate her. It serves as a sedative, which allows the process to take place. She is known to be the only Jinni that copulates with human males and was despised by her Jinni race.

I am told by an elderly lady that her secrete was unearthed by a young couple who for some odd reason were never affected by field of force that she surrounded herself while it petrified and blinded others. The elders believe it to be a challenge from her father.

This couple choused such mundane place for romantic rendezvoused. They were so immersed in passion and love that jina Nyima was deliriously delighted watching them carry on, kiss, laugh, act frisky, mischievous, and at times crying over each other's shoulders.

The jinni was amorous and affixed by the pantomime that unfolds before her from humanoids in love. In this panoply of a paradoxical state paralleled to none the pariah queen jinni is entertained. It represented a cavalcade of paroxysms in her life.

In one hand should instantly those invading her territory instantly into stones. On the other she rendered this couple immune to her spell for they were source of joy and relief from normal jinni panoplies.

It was a parody by which this pariah jinni takeoff her shoulders cumbersome load imposed upon her by Jinni

Musa. To make certain of this entertainment, which by the way varies daily, that always left her heart laden with love, envy, and a wish she too was a human instead of the jinni race she belonged she favored as well spared them the effect of her spell around Bere Kolong.

Some villagers reported that the Jinni queen and her human lover do at times change into human forms and adorned the most fancy dresses and join the villagers in their festivities, christenings, thanks giving, and even during burial rites.

This jinni was one with human heart encased in a spirit that refuses to be with its kind. At the same time if any human makes the wrong move to wooing her mate she is dealt with immediately. How do the innocent distinguish this icy hand of the stone hedges from real people?

It so happens that one look at the couple reveals the tell tales of uniqueness not seen in any in the gathering. They looked perfect in features, youthful despite notable advancing age, they still retain teenage voices, and they behave very maturely while saying very little at all.

They are normally interested in the elderly and children but maintain short conversations with them. Hence this attribute leaves people suspicious and circumspect at all times when such figurines are in attendants. Above all, one or two well respected oracle or soothsayers would normally issue warnings to the likely hood that the couple may per chance appear at such gatherings well before the chosen date of the function. However, their presence was never the dooms day or as bleak as the oracles normally predicts.

At the middle or end of each function the jinni couple donates bags upon bags of money and clothing to the organizers and villagers leaving everyone happy and in welcoming spirit. The only missing part of the jigsaw is that there is that neither a village nor known address exists for this philanthropic couple.

Amazingly all the villagers' notice at the end of visit is sudden appearance of power cyclone marking their disappearance to Batutadou before eventually returning to Bere Kolong.

In the end the villagers learnt to live with this phenomenon and those who bore baby boys leave the environment believing that might safe their from being kidnapped by the jinni.

They run to neighbors and relatives at villages hundreds of miles away until their child matures. I am told that this activity of kidnapping and breeding with ceased males continued for millenniums until one night when a ball of fire was seen to rise to the sky leaving behind it row after row of petrified and chard stones in human form or figurines surrounding Bere Kolong.

Some believe it to mark the death of the queen jinni daughter of Jina Musa. Up to today visitors to Bere Kolong could see stones, in similar fashion to the stone hedges, standing alongside the great Bere Kolong. Some observers reported spotting one or two tears weeping while other figurines drone a smile at beholders.

All in all and unto the present time no villager dares draw water from Bere Kolong for fear of angering the mutant jinni she left behind. One good thing about the place is that modern day man had taken advantage and has turned the well into a tourist Mecca generating revenue for the villages and the region.

This then was the gift from the most bazaar romantic affair between jinni and man. The saying all is well that ends well hold true for this story the queen jinni love.

READERS KINDLY ALLOW ME DIGRESS TO NATTY GERITY WHY THIS BOOK.

Chapter 18

A SUCCESSFUL MAN LEARNS FROM HIS MISTAKES

All humans make mistakes or are capable of making one. The difference in outcome of our errors is being able to accept that we erred and to learn from it to make better judgments next time. Some say my mistake was refusing to stay in the village mould and that I was too ambitious if not a grandiose psychopath pursuing Western ideals.

So far, I have been able to assail through most criticisms and completed university education despite it all. Some say I should not have left America to study medicine at A. M. Dogliotti, school of medicine in Monrovia, Liberia, West Africa or even attend the American university of the Caribbean at Montserrat in the West Indies.

Friends have on many occasions asked why I did not seek the Green card while a student in America or apply for the United Kingdom citizenship during my clinical clerkship rotation at Colchester, Essex. My response then and even today is that I refrained from such a course because I love Africa and there is no place I rather be other than the Gambia.

More over our people need our services more than any other place. I love helping villagers and would do just that with my life in the time that God gave me on planet earth. In addition I am certain to fulfill my goal, with help of Manding Medical Centre, of providing medical aid to the villager. The end result of, dear reader, that error, if it be one, was it turned me into the doctor I am today for the villagers and the needy. The road to that lofty end was long and difficult at times too slippery and steep to walk on. It was strewed with stagnation, starvation, and destitutions life.

Hope you will agree that the end result was worth the means for family and country. It is no fanfare or path for the weak and none persistent person. I suffered tremendously since my arrival in the UK, the so-called land of honey and milk of Europe.

I faced series of evictions from flats, had been threatened with CCJ actions and a host of collection agents vying to lay hands on anything belonging to me to recoup money owed to either the RBS or BT. Life in this state was nerving, shameful and painful.

The mistake, which lead to this disheartening state, was that I came to the UK on a visitor's visa. The Home Office's refusal to reclassify my visa to a student visa landed me into hell on earth. Some asked if the struggle was worth the pain and dehumanization state I found myself at.

My response had always been a resounding yes with a challenge for doubters to meet me in the Gambia upon my completing certification with the GMC three years hence.

On my way home, I had two fellows discussing about me. The other said that I was wrong in not listening as well as obeying my father's wish that I become a farmer instead of being immersed in some foreign ideology and system. The sensible one retorted by asking why they were the in UK and not farming in the Gambia.

He told his companion that Dr. Ceesay was spending himself for the future good of all Gambians for if his medical center catches on it would be added valuable medical service to the Gambia and the Badibus in particular. I met some Gambian at the Alexandra Park and they too suggested that think of returning since life had been nothing but a downward spiral for me since my coming to the UK.

I reminded them that if mountain climbers were scared of the height they wish conquered or mistakes others made in their attempts to climb those mountains, we would never assailed Mount Everest. A mistake is a necessary lesson to learn from and to humble ourselves from the belief of being infallible. Our mistakes are eye openers to bigger gains.

They may at first be bitter to swallow but if we learn from them we gain a lot of insight in future plans. If the Manding Medical Centre and all it now provide the Gambia was a mistake then I pray to make a billion more similar sincere mistakes for mankind.

It is said to err is human and to forgive divine. I hope those could not see beyond the tip of their noses could forgive me for refusing to stay in the village mould and pursue to the hilt what I believe to be worthy end for the Gambia, villagers and the downtrodden.

I am no angel and like you I am full of human imperfections. The difference between my critics and I is that I am a dreamer who never gives up dreaming and I am always ready to see the dreams come true to a positive beneficial reality for all of us.This is my way of leaving footprints on the sand of time so that beleaguered Gambians can muster courage and work for the development of the region.

It is my hope that Manding Medical Centre continues to be the template its today for generations to come. Let us learn from our mistakes and have the foresight and fortitude to turn them into something positive for all. Grandpa Bajoja advised that we have courage to accept our faults and fortitude to correct them for the good of all. The world is not always our making but we must make the best of it.

Chapter 19

PRISONER OF MY AMBITION FOR THE VILLAGER

The burning embers of a wish and hope for my people became a prison wall that kept caving onto me any time I relaxed my effort. Ambition to bring the golden Flees, in the form of medical aid, to the villager constantly hunts me and reminds me of my covenant for the Gambia. There were no doubts in my mind that I was rightfully engaged in bringing much needed medical service to the region served by Manding Medical Centre in the Gambia.

I literally became the fugue of the family as I pushed to bring my desire to provide proper medical aid into fruition for the villager in the North Bank of the Gambia. This quest for a better medical service to neglected villagers led to my disappearing from the family horizon to America as early as 1967.

There I started the challenge of my life in a drive to become a doctor of medicine serving the Gambia. The path of this adventure is well documented in my first book, "The legend against all odds" published by Publish America, Baltimore, Maryland, USA in August 2002.

The strength of my conviction along with a mindset to do something concrete for my people made me give up today's pleasures for a better tomorrow for the Gambia. An Armchair psychologist, Dr. Kube Lonna (nick named

Dr. Hamham), once told me. "Dreamers are a pain in the neck". I asked why? And he replied, "They wake up with one of the most ridiculous ideas and try not only to live in that nonsense but implement them for the rest of their lives. Us pragmatics and wise become skeptical and weary of the dreamer and brand him either a total loony or living in a planet by himself or herself".

I replied quoting Lawrence of Arabia. Who said "All men dream: but not equally. Those who dream by the night in the dusty recesses of their minds wake in the day to find that it was vanity; but the dreamers of the day are dangerous men, for they act their dream with open eyes to make it possible."

I further made it clear that none the less many dreamers have converts. I asked what converts the sage to the dreamer' path? To this he gave the most amazing reply in favour of the dreamers and people with strong convictions like mine.

My armchair psychologist told me, "We only become flabbergasted as the dream unfolds to bits of reality opening up wide realms unknown to us before that day". He continued by illustrating what he meant. "Take for example the case of the Rights brothers and their attempt to fly. Boy oh boy!

Some critics who strongly believed that only birds, goblins, and angels had the privilege of flight ridiculed the Rights brothers as witches. Today you and I know better for we now use the Rights brother's dream to fly round the world at ease and by it we have catapulted to the moon and beyond".

I hope this has cleared the air for the reader as to why some of us are considered as whacks and a challenge to my friend the sage armchair psychologist Dr. Kube Lonna. Very early in my high school days friends labelled me as a reclusive person not knowing that my whole psyche was based on going aboard and becoming one of the future doctors of the Gambia.

I am fully aware of all work and no play not only turns us into monsters but also indeed a very dull one at that. I just moderated my life and made certain that I never lost track of my direction in life and my ambition for the Gambian villager.

After ten years in America my family considered me being lost in zealous desire to gain book knowledge or Western education. I learnt that my father, while on his deathbed urged that prayers be offered so that I, the family fugue would return home. Like Marco Polo or Sinbad's adventures mine had seen me fly on several times to America, Liberia, the West Indies and the United Kingdom seeking more skills with which to serve my people. It is said that life is lonely at the top but I found it even lonelier when struggling from ground zero with no hope of financial assistance at sight. Every hour of my life had to be organized in a way to minimize loss of income and to maintain progress in my academic pursuits.

Hence I worked on three jobs during the summer breaks and at school libraries to raise funds for my education or repayment of loans which enable me continue schooling.To me every ounce of energy and any cent spent on my aspiration to become a doctor in the Gambia was as exhilarating as becoming an overnight multimillionaire. It is a joy I wish I could share with you. Graduating from medical school and my first patient in the Gambia are indelible blessed moments I hold dear to my heart. The rewards will forever be for my people and humanity.

Chapter 20

DISTIGUISHED 2005 GRADUATE AWARD

TO DR. Alhasan CEESAY

I attended Alpena Community College (ACC) in Michigan, USA, from September 1967 to December 1979. My contact with friends at Alpena never waned. Hence the wheels of profound recognition by the institute started rolling when Mathew Dunckel called me to let me know he read my book, "The Legend against All Odds".

He was very impressed and intrigued by my experience and fortitude since my leaving Alpena Community College in 1979. I met Mathew when he was twelve years old. His father Dr. Elbridge Dunckle was my academic advisor while I was at Alpena community College. I will without any reservation still recommend Dr. Dunckel for academic advisor to any foreign student attending the college.

It was during one of our telephone conversation (02/01/05) that Mathew told me of the possibility of ACC recommending me for the Distinguished 2005 Graduate award offered annually by Alpena Community College to its outstanding Alumni. Alpena Community College foundation recognizes its graduates annually for their academic and their career accomplishment for their communities. It simply recognizes the aspirations of

Alumni for their people. The Pandora's Box was opened by innocuous telephone conversation in recognizing my aspiration and goal for providing medical aid to Gambian villagers. Mathew asked me to fax him any and all possible documentation about me and work I do in the Gambia.

He would then speak to the relevant authorities regarding my being nominated for the Distinguished 2005 graduate of Alpena Community College coming May 5th 2005 spring/summer commencement. Mathew did just as promised. In a nutshell, here is the letter from Mrs. Penny Boldrey, Executive Director Alpena Community College Foundation. It read:-

Alpena Community College

666 Johnson Street

Alpena, MI 49707

January 6, 2005

Alhasan S. Ceesay, MD

245 Great Western Street

Manchester M14 4LQ

England

Dear Dr. Ceesay,

Mathew Dunckel shared the information that you recently provided to him regarding your professional achievements since your early years at Alpena Community College. I'm extremely pleased to share with you that your many outstanding accomplishments have earned you the distinction of Distinguished Graduate of Alpena Community College (ACC) for 2005.

We commend you for your humanitarian efforts in founding and developing the Manding Medical Centre in Gambia, West Africa. I'm anxious to read your book. "The legend against all odds" once Matt has finished with it. Without a doubt, you serve as an example of how a solid educational foundation from Alpena Community College can launch a lifetime of achievements.

You will be honored at our spring commencement exercises on Thursday, May 5, which begins at 7 pm, in the Park Arena at ACC. We invite you to join us on that evening. However, we certainly understand that making a trip to the United States, on so short a notice, may not be feasible. During the commencement program, I will share a synopsis of your extraordinary career that has earned you the honour of Distinguished Graduate.

If you are able to join us, you will be invited to join me at the podium to receive your award and to address the audience if you wish. Would you be willing to provide us with the following: 1) a copy of your professional resume; 2) a paragraph on your memories of ACC and how your experience helped you achieve your goals; 3) a professional photo for use in our alumni newsletter as well as in an ad that will appear in Alpena news.

 Please feel free to call me or e-mail me with any additional questions you may have. Again, congratulations! We look forward to hearing from you in the future.

Sincerely

Penny Boldrey

Executive Director

My response to this honour and invitation to my second home America was swift and obvious as penned bellow. I e-mailed Penny forth with as my heart was overwhelmed by joy for being recognized by my Alma Mata ACC. It simply stated:-

13/01/05,

Manchester, UK.

Dear Penny Boldrey,

I am overwhelmed and do not know where to begin this note of thanks to Alpena Community College. In my mind it's the American people who deserve such honour and distinction for I am only recipient of the goodness of the

Americans. I am humbled and further rejuvenated by the thought and recognition of my goals and work for the Gambia. I remember in the 60s when people used to tell me, "You will end up just like all foreign students who came to America.

They end up getting trapped by the greener pasture syndrome of America." To such challenges my response had always been; I for one will disappoint a lot of you for I will never rest until I bring to my people the American know how and willingness to share with others.

This stance has never changed and will not ever change because the only way I can, in a small measure compared to what you did for us poor ones, pay back is to be able to show what the USA is all about and her stand for the little guy anywhere on this planet.

I will look into my schedule to see if I can afford to be in Alpena May 2005. I will let you know by the end of February 2005. Mean while I'm faxing a resume and will try to send my photos by e-mail.

Where it is not possible for me to attend in May, would it be okay for my first Alpena family friend, Mrs. Rita Riggs to represent me at the ACC' spring Commencement Ceremony. She was the first people in Alpena that opened their homes to me.

She and her family will certainly appreciate recognition of their help to this simple Gambian. None the less rest assured that I have not yet slammed the door to my seeing Alpena once more. Timing and visa problems might make it unattainable.

Again, please accept profound gratitude to all of you and to Alpena Community College. God blesses you and rain peace on earth in 2005. Cheers and regards.

Sincerely

Dr. Alhasan S. Ceesay

My lovely daughter: Binta Ceesay

Mrs. Boldrey replied thus:

ACC, Michigan 49707

13/01/05

Hi Dr. Ceesay,

Yes, I did receive your curriculum vitae and thank you for forwarding that to me! We are extremely proud of you and your accomplishments! Once I get my hand on your book, I will pay special notice to the ACC chapter. The best part of my job is the opportunity to meet former alumni and learn of the impact ACC had in their lives.

Please believe me that we understand if you are unable to join us at commencement on May 5. Indeed we would be pleased to have Rita Riggs accept this honour on your behalf. Rita is remarkable and kind woman. My husband speaks fondly of her and has stayed in close contact with her. I look forward to getting to know you better through our correspondence! And meet you in person someday. Regards

Its

Mrs. Penny Boldrey

Executive Director

At the end it was not possible for me to attend the ceremony in person. So Rita Riggs and her family stepped in for me. Her elder son Robert Riggs was designated to receive the award in my behalf as representative of Rita who was in her 80s at the time. I emailed the follow short remarks to be read by Robert Riggs at the time the award is given. It is titled:-

A FUTURE FOR ALL

Mr. President, staff, Graduates, Ladies and Gentlemen; I am deeply moved and humbled being chosen Alpena Community College's Distinguished Alumni for 2005.This recognition belongs to America. Without the good will and foresight of the staff, students and the community of Alpena in 1967, I might never have had the chance to earn education with which to help my people move forward in life.

Hence, allow me reiterate profound gratitude to Alpena Community College, my fellow students, people of Alpena and America at large. My life after Alpena has been full of trials and tribulations detailed in my first book, "The legend against all odds". One relief in it is the robust blessing and peace of mind I have knowing that I am right in what I am doing for my people.

There are those who claim Heaven in being rich but for me it is reaching out to help others that matters in life. Upon graduating from medical school, I returned to the

Gambia and setup a self-help village Health organization (Manding Medical Centre) at Njawara village in an effort to provide a much needed medical service to the rural sector. I am happy to report that membership has grown beyond twenty thousand villagers.

Please join me to catch a dream for my villagers. Manding medical centre will help portray the America we all dream of and yearn to be part. We are on the verge of building the children's unit and do need monetary, equipment and medicines assistance in our drive to provide this unique service to villagers.

To the graduates, I would like to remind you that, the great tide of history flows and as it flows it carries to the shores of reality what binds us as one human race. Be aware of the extent, depth and gravity of the challenges ahead as you set out to transform, reconstruct and integrate America into a global icon.

Sincere congratulations for your march towards success and fulfillment. Alpena Community College has given you the first footprints. Walk your way with head held high and determination to succeed in the world.

Confucius said, "Our greatest glory is never failing, but in rising every time we fail." Stockpiles of atomic bombs or weapons of mass destruction and dictators do not measure greatness.

I believe strongly and sincerely that with deep-rooted wisdom and dignity, innate respect for human right and lives, the intense humanity will make us more cherished and better leaders. This will make us able to contribute towards the future and progress of mankind. I am happy for you and hope that you will fly the American flag for it is the great American constitution.

Finally, I would like to pay tribute to pass and present staff, students of ACC and Alpena community for having given me the opportunity to forge for my people. Allow me make special mention and express thanks to the remarkable and noble friends I met in Alpena.

Sincere thanks from my family, villagers and I to Howard & Rita Rigg, Judge Philip & Viola S. Glennie, Mr. Henry V. Valli, Dr. Elbridge Dunckel, Dr. Strom, Bill & Magritte Cruise, Dr. Charles T. Egli and the Alpena medical association, Mr. Cloyd Ramsey & the Medical Arts Clinic and all who helped make my sojourn to Alpena a remarkable success. If I have a million friends, I would like many more to be like you. I hope you will believe in, as well as join me, in my dream of providing modern medical aid to the Gambian villagers. Thanks a million and God bless America!

BY: DR. ALHASAN SISAWO CEESAY, MD

Mrs. Penny Boldrey called to let me know she confirmed the details with Robert Rigg, who was selected by the family to deliver the speech. She assured me that Bob was all set with my remarks and had been practicing many times. Rita and Donna will also be attending with other friends. To make it official she sent this note to Robert Rigg (Bob).

April 21, 2005

Robert Rigg

312 Liberty Street

Alpena, MI 49707

Dear Bob,

Dr. Alhasan Ceesay has informed that you will be representing him at our commencement ceremony and accepting the Distinguished Graduate Award on his behalf. Our spring commencement exercises will be held on Thursday, May 5, at 7 pm.

There will be VIP seating near the front left section of the Park Arena for and your family. During the commencement program, I will share a brief synopsis of Dr. Ceesay's career.

I will invite you to join me at the podium to receive Dr. Ceesay's Distinguished Graduate Award. Following the presentation, you will have the opportunity to share Dr. Ceesay's remarks. I shared with Dr. Ceesay that his comments must be kept brief (2-3 minutes) because our program consist of many individuals who will also be addressing the graduating class.

After the ceremony we would like to take some photographs, so if you could remain near your seats, I will come to you. A reception at the Jeese Besser Museum follows commencement and you are also invited to join. Enclosed you will find a copy of Dr. Ceesay's remarks. I look forward to hearing from you. Please call me to confirm your participation.

Sincerely

Penny Boldrey

Executive Director

Two weeks prior to the ceremony I received an e-mail letting me know that Karen Eller, administrative assistant in the president's (ACC) office of Public information will be writing about me in the Lumberjack Link spring /summer alumni newsletter publication.

Penny also told me that Kerrie Miller (also alumni) and news writer for The Alpena News would like to feature me in the local paper.

I immediate e-mailed the following to Kerrie Miller at the Alpena News. Hi Kerrie, I just received Penny's email with the good news that you want to feature me in the Alpena News. For me this would be a dream come true. Yes! By all means go ahead and feel free to contact me should you want more information about me or the work I'm doing in the Gambia.

I am a simple person that loves to help others get on with life the best way they can during their short sojourn on mother earth. I strongly believe that house of us who had the privilege to learn from America have responsibility to share American goodwill with our people.

That is the only way they, our people, can experience the real America that stands for the down trodden and the innovative. I still feel very happy when come across an American. If your paper is able to help me get Manding Medical Centre at Njawara out of its current limbo, then you would have participated in the most noble and worthy course that will outlive us and will be a spring board of hope and medical service for generations we can ever dream of.

It is my daughter Binta Ceesay

We are still on fund raising stage to build the first phase, the children's unit, which according to estimates will cost around £250,000 or about $500,000 dollars. I committed all proceeds of my book, "The legend against all odds", to the centre but it is not selling enough to get things in fast gear.

I need help to bring relief to my villagers. Well, this is enough introductions until I hear from you. God bless you and thanks a million for being kind towards us.

Sincerely

Dr. Alhasan S. Ceesay

Kerrie Miller replied and asked that I send her a synopsis of how I found out Alpena in the 60s. So I sent her the following summary. "I came to be in Alpena by simply going to the then American Consulate in Banjul, the Gambia and asked for a catalogue with information on American colleges.

As a beggar normally has no choice, I started from the top alphabets. Well, Alpena Community college was there and was the first that accepted my application among the schools that replied to my desire to pursue further education in America.

This part is well expanded in chapter in my book "The legend against all odds" highlighting my experience at ACC from 1967 -1969. I was born and bread in abject poverty and I'm only fighting for my villagers to have a chance to proper medical care etc, etc nothing more and nothing -less.

I hope you will help get your readers interested in Manding Medical Centre and its objective for the villagers. Thank you for taking upon the task of writing about me and my work in the Gambia. Manding Medical Centre is in limbo and we year for a boost or a short in the arm to get things moving faster. Please visit our website: www.Friends of manding gambimed.com

It's

Dr. A. Ceesay

I will later reproduce both articles written by Karen Eller for the Lumberjack Link and Kerrie Miller's in the Alpena News respectively. For now let us head to the spring commencement podium and listen to what Mrs. Penny Boldrey has in mind about this simple village doctor. Bob and his family attended in time and it was now time for Penny's remarks about my achievements from the days of Alpena Community College to now.

It is simple and movingly started thus:-

"Good evening and congratulations graduates!

The Alpena Community College Foundation created the Distinguished Graduate award not only to recognize, but to honour our graduates who have gone on to contribute to society through successful careers. Our recipient tonight serves as an example of how a solid education foundation from ACC can launch a lifetime of achievements.

I 'm pleased to share with you that our 2005 Distinguished Graduate is Dr. Alhasan Ceesay from the Gambia, West Africa. Dr Ceesay received his Associates of Arts Degree in 1969, exactly two years after leaving the Gambia.

He credits many individuals, and the generosity of others, as the driving force behind his success. Following his graduation from ACC, Dr. Ceesay transferred to Olivet College, on a full-tuition scholarship provided to him by the Besser Foundation. In 1971, he earned a Bachelor of Arts Degree in Biology from Olivet, and in 1973 completed his Master of Science degree from Michigan Technological University at Houghton Michigan, USA. Dr. Ceesay taught biology for several years in the Gambia before entering into medical school in 1992, he was awarded his Doctor of Medicine Degree from the American University of the Caribbean.

Dr. Ceesay again returned to the Gambia, and provided free medical assistance to the villagers for an entire year before he took a position as House Officer at the Royal Victoria Hospital, Banjul, the Gambia, and was eventually promoted to the post of Medical Officer in 1999.

He is the proud founder of the Manding Medical Centre, a self-help village Health organisation located in the Gambia, which has provided much needed medical care to over 8000 villagers. In his autobiography, "The legend Against All Odds", Dr. Ceesay shares his struggle to survive in his quest for an education. All the proceeds from his book go to supporting the Manding Medical Centre.

Dr. Ceesay and his wife have three daughters, ages 14, 11 and 7. In my correspondence with Dr. Ceesay over the past few months, he shared his profound gratitude for his American education.

He said, "In my mind, it is the American who deserved such honour and distinction, for I'm the recipient of the goodness of the Americans." Due to travel difficulties, Dr. Ceesay is unable to be here tonight to accept this award. However he has asked his first American family, the Howard Rigg family to represent him.

At this time I'll ask Bob Rigg to join me at the podium to accept the award for Dr. Ceesay. Indeed, it is truly an honour to recognize Dr. Ceesay for his many accomplishments and humanitarian efforts. We congratulate him on earning the Distinction of Distinguished Graduate of Alpena Community College. – Penny Boldrey-

Robert Rigg eloquently delivered my remarks aimed at the graduates and residents of Alpena city. It was welcomed as I was later told by those who were able to e-mail me. Alpena city and ACC were very happy. This Distinguished Graduate award came thirty 36 odd years since I last visited Alpena, Michigan.

Mathew Dunckel sent me the following comments about the evening of the award. "Alhasan, your address was given at commencement. It was the portion of the evening that was enjoyed by most. Partly because it was delivered well and partly because of my father was mentioned. I think what you said was inspirational for our students and brought home the need for them to think internationally.

Tom Ray is making final preparation to depart for Gambia early next week. What a great adventure for the students. I am looking forward to hearing about it on their return. Thank you for helping make it happen.

Your friend

Matt.

I sent Penny Boldrey the following; "I received both the award and enclosures. Accept my deepest appreciation for the kind words spoken about me in your presentation speech during the spring graduation ceremony. Thank you very much for your kindness."

I suggested we pursue the possibility of twining Alpena with two villages in the Gambia. Dear reader, I hope your patience is not running out as you eagerly look forward to the publication for alumni and friends of Alpena Community College.

Karen Eller wrote to let me know that she was assigned to write a news article for the local paper announcing my receiving the Distinguished Graduate award. She read my book, "The legend against all odds," to garner more information about me to help her on the matter at hand. She continued by letting me know that she found my story very interesting and she intend to do a good job at the article.

Here without further ado is Karen Eller's article about me. This idea unfolded to reality in the chapter on sister city proclamation.

THE LUMBERJACK LINK: ALPENA MICHIGAN

DR. CEESAY NAMED DISTINGUISHED GRADUATE

Dr. Alhasan Sisawo Ceesay of the Gambia, West Africa, was recognized with the Distinguished Graduate award at the ACC spring commencement ceremony in May 5th, 2005. On hand to receive the award for Dr. Ceesay was members of the Howard Rigg family, his first host family when he came to Alpena in 1967.

According to Dr. Ceesay, "The Riggs were the ideal American, an average working class who readily shared the little bit God gave them with others less fortunate." Dr. Ceesay earned his Associate of Arts degree from ACC in 1969 and went on to Olivet College to earn his Bachelor's degree in biology with the help of a full-tuition scholarship from the Besser Foundation.

He earned his Master's degree in biological sciences from Michigan Technological University in 1973. In 1979, Dr. Ceesay returned to Africa and entered the University of Liberia Medical School in Monrovia.

Because of political unrest in the Gambia in 1981, Dr. Ceesay escaped to the United States in hopes of completing his lifelong dream; "to provide medical relief to the villager who is forced to walk miles on end to seek medical aid for his already dying child, wife or friend."

During the time he was seeking political asylum in the United States, Dr. Ceesay never gave up his quest for education, and he continued to take classes at Michigan State University and Wayne State University. He was finally accepted at the American University of the Caribbean in the West Indies, and he began the final segment of his journey to becoming a doctor. In 1992, after 25 years of educational struggles, Dr. Ceesay was awarded his Doctor of Medicine degree from the American University of the Caribbean. He returned to the Gambia where he provided free medical assistance to the villagers for an entire year before taking a position at the Royal Victoria Hospital, Banjul, The Gambia.

Dr. Ceesay founded Manding Medical Centre in 1993. This is a self-help village health organization which provides much needed medical aid to the villagers of the Gambia, West Africa.

His autobiography, "The legend against all odds," chronicles his struggle to survive in his quest for Western education. Proceeds of his book go to support Manding Medical Centre at Njawara village and provide scholarships in medicine and agriculture for indigent rural candidates in the Gambia. To learn more about Dr. Ceesay's ambitions, you can e-mail him at alhasanceesay@hotmail.com.

Dr. Ceesay was honoured to receive this distinction from ACC and would like to "express thanks to the remarkable and noble friends" he met in Alpena. He credits the goodwill and foresight of the staff and students at ACC for giving him the chance to earn an education and help move his people forward in life.

-Karen Eller-

I thank Karen Eller for this revealing commendable article. Here now is that featured by the Alpena News written by news staff Kerrie L. Miller. This is Miller's version about me and my goals.

ALPENA NEWS, MICHIGAN, USA 2005 A LONG ROAD FROM GAMBIA TO ALPENA

When he was about 14, Dr. Alhasan S. Ceesay saw a family tragedy unfold that would change his life forever. As he was walking to school, he saw a woman, pregnancy full-term, who was obviously ill. Her husband was carrying their young son who was nearly comatose from illness.

Ceesay later found out the pregnant woman's baby died in uterus and she died from the toxins built up in her body as a result. The young boy also died three quarters of a mile before his family was able to reach the health centre at Kerewan village.

"That day I said, "If God will help me, no one will ever have to go through that again. That picture is what made up my mind for me," Ceesay said. Ceesay, a native of Njawara, Gambia, is a graduate of Alpena Community College, class of 1969.

He earned his Associate's of Arts degree from ACC before attending Olivet College, Michigan Tech and Howard University, earning his doctor of medicine degree from the America University of the Caribbean in 1992.

But how does a young man from a village in Gambia get to Alpena to attend its community college? In an e-mail message, he stated that after reaching the American Consulate, and asking for a listing of American colleges, Alpena Community College was at the top of the alphabetical list.

And Acc was the first to respond to his application. Once here, life was not without challenges. In a telephone conversation, he said it was the first time he had left his country, and when he got here no one spoke his language. "But I don't give up," he said. Another goal Ceesay never gave up on was making it possible for village families, such as those like the one who affected him as deeply as a young man, to have access to health care services.

With the creation of the Manding Medical Centre, which has helped over 8000 patients free of charge, he is doing that. Though progress has been very slow in coming to the centre; Ceesay said officially he is employed by the central government and is only on the weekends is he able to man the centre, along with three or four other doctors who volunteer their time.

Ceesay say the centre sees no fewer than 500 patients and as many as 1,500 patients in a weekend. He said currently the centre is in limbo and is a little more than a shed.

He has been working on fund-raising to get the first phase, a children's unit, built. It is expected to cost approximately $500,000. Members of the ACC Leadership Class are currently conducting fund-raising to go to Gambia and help with the children and volunteering at the centre. The trip will last two weeks.

Ceesay is the author of a book chronicling his life's experiences called "The legend against all odds" (available at Amazon .com) and he has committed all proceeds of its sale to the centre. He said he's never regretted the decision he made to become a doctor. "Sometimes I feel like I have oil on my feet and I'm climbing a very steep hill."

Ceesay said. "I have always believed I'll reach my goal… you have to be crazy like me and you have to ignore lots of things that take you away from your goals." A typical day in Ceesay's life begins at 5 am with prayer, before boarding public transportation to the hospital where he works, 7 miles from his home. From 7 – 11 am he does morning rounds, followed by clinics, then evening rounds.

Days can last up to 10 or 11 pm before he heads back home. "In between, I try to please my wife and children. It's a very simple life really," he said. He and his wife have three daughters, the oldest of which has dreams of attending Alpena High School and ACC before going onto medical school like her father. Ceesay's long-term goals revolve around the medical centre, which he hopes will continue to grow for generations, helping thousands more patients. "I plan to stay at the centre until the day they bury me. That and have my children educated. That's it," he said.

-Kerrie Miller-

Kerrie sent me a copy of the Alpena news. And I sent the following in appreciation of the good work in the article. Kerrie, I just received a copy of the Alpena news featuring me. It was a job well done.

I hope it help move my dream of providing medical aid to villagers a notch higher for Manding Medical centre and the Gambian villagers. The Gambia and I are most grateful for enlightening your readers about us and our need for a medical facility.

Extend our thanks and deep appreciation to the staff and Alpena-news. We shall definitely be in Gambia in due course. We look forward to your crew attending the ground breaking ceremonies in Gambia soon.

I have started a collection of documentations about me to be placed in Dr. Alhasan S. Ceesay's achieves. Kerrie Miller replied saying that they missed me for the ceremony but she look forward to attending the grand opening of the centre.

Penny Boldrey simply said, "I will certainly make sure you receive a copy of our alumni newsletter once it's completed. Indeed, we are very proud of your accomplishments and humanitarian efforts."

Mrs. Fatou Koma Ceesay, Oldham, UK, 2017

Chapter 21

The telephone call on 5/01/05 from Mr. Mathew Dunckel as well as that from Mr. Thomas Ray (TOM) four days later opened the Pandora's box and became harbingers to a remarkable trip to Manding Medical Centre, Njawara village, Gambia by the Alpena Community College's Leadership class headed by none other than their instructor Mr. Thomas P. Ray.

I contacted Mr. Thomas Ray as soon as it was brought to my attention that some ACC students were contemplating visiting my centre at Njawara in May 2005. My message on the 6/01/05 to Mr. Ray ran thus:-

"An old friend, Mr. Mathew, staff of ACC, had a long chat with me last night and he brought to my attention of a possibility that a class wanting to travel to the Gambia as guest of Manding Medical Centre at Njawara. I am more than willing and happy to pave the way for those that would venture the trip.

I do need an e-mail or fax from you indicating desire to go to the Gambia on a mission for Manding Medical Centre. I will speak to both the schools and the district authority about your most welcomed trip to the Gambia.

Manding Medical Centre is a self-help village health organization I setup in upon returning to the Gambia in1992. We provide medical service to villagers and land has been donated for the location of the centre and its ancillaries. We only have a corrugated shed as clinic.

We are now on the verge of building the first phase, being the children's unit of the centre and need monetary assistance. I am delighted to know of your intentions. Please contact me as soon as you speak with the class."

Thomas Ray replied on 7/01/05, "I was thrilled when Mathew discussed the possibility of a trip to Gambia for our leadership students. I will meet with the whole class next week to discuss the possibility.

As I am sure you are aware the cost of airfares from Alpena to Gambia is high, so I will need to be certain the students are committed to raising the money needed before we begin making plans.

I have travelled to many locations, but never to Africa, so I am also very excited about the prospects for myself. After I meet with the students on Tuesday of next week, I will e-mail you with further information. I wish to also commend you for your personal achievements; I plan to purchase a copy of your recent book to share with my students and for my personal reading. Thank you for your help and enthusiasm."

I emailed Tom advising that to bargain for insured group tickets. Tom further contacted me on 12/01/05 stating that he has spoken to the students and they have agreed to take on a service trip as part of the course. He told me that they would only be able to travel in a group for 10 – 14 days in May 2005.

Tom wanted to know if there was an existing program at Njawara that would be able to accommodate the students. He assured me that the students would be comfortable in a dormitory housing or make shift dormitories.

In addition I let him know on the 14/01/05 that I have spoken to the commissioner, North Bank Division and the local authority in Lower Badibou district regarding their pending trip to Njawara as guest of Manding Medical Centre and the region.

I assured him that these authorities would be more than happy to have his class visit with them. I requested an e-mail from him stating that they are visiting in behalf of Manding Medical Centre at Njawara and specify what they would want to do while in the Gambia. I suggested that they can help teach in some of the schools.

I assured them that even though business and some residents have moved out there is still some activity at the village. Tom in reply sent the following on the 15/01/05. "Thank you for the great news.

I am very excited about the prospect and have begun searching for group airfares with special student rates. I will inform the students on Tuesday and contact you immediately afterward via email. I have a few questions. What costs do we need to expect in Gambia and in your village?

How will we travel from Banjul to the village? We need to be certain we have a clear idea what expenses we will have to help us set specific fundraising goals both for ourselves and for the foundation from which we hope to receive grants. When I write the other e-mail, are there tasks other than tutoring that I should include? Are there other ways we can help while we are there?

I am more excited about the prospect of this service trip everyday and the students are quite enthused." In another e-mail dated 15/02/05, Tom wrote, "The students in the leadership class are so committed to this project that they voted to contribute their own money toward the travel if they cannot raise enough.

This means that the number of students who actually travel will likely be fewer, but that we will be able to travel to Njawara in May. I have begun drafting the letter to the commissioner many times, but I have some questions. Am I asking the commissioner to help organise local housing for us?

Do I want his permission to visit Njawara? Should I tell him what we would like to do there? What subject might they tutor? Are there any construction projects for the centre or the village with which we could help?

I would also like to know if there are any material supplies we could bring with us to donate to the centre or the village. One possible way for us to save money would be to fly into Dakar, Senegal and travel from there overland to Njawara.

All the above concerns and questions were answered but a small hiccup in fundraising occurred leaving a distinct possibility that the students will not be able to raise enough to make the trip.

The reason being the major source of funding for the trip fell through. This left all of us jittery but Tom and his students were in no mood to change their plans to travel to the Gambia in May 2005. On the same day 15/02/05 I received the following from Mr. Jay Walterriet, Director of Public information for Alpena Community College. It stated that he was asked to contact me for more photos of myself and the clinic at Njawara.

He wanted more information regarding the Leadership planned trip to Gambia. I was told that the local television station would like to do a segment on the Leadership class and their trip. As part of the segment photos were needed.

I sent all photos that were relevant to enable the reporter to do his TV-segment on the planned Leadership trip to Njaswara, Gambia. Mr. Jay on the 17/02/05 emailed thanking me for providing the requested photos and assured me that ACC has received good deal of interest from the local media regarding the Leadership class trip and both he and Penny Boldrey were trying to provide all of the information they could.

My e-mail was given to reporters who might want to contact me for more information. The entire twenty students could not enlist for the final take off to Africa. So Thomas Ray and 11 students took on the venture of their life time to the Gambia as guest of Manding Medical Centre at Njawara village.

On 17 February 2005 Tom sent me a copy of the final letter he sent to the commissioner and the local authority at the Lower Badibou district spelling out their intentions and wish while guests of the Manding Medical Centre for a two weeks duration. Here it is.

Thomas P. Ray

Alpena Community College

666 Johnson Street

Alpena, Michigan 49707

17 February 2005

Dear Commissioner Batala Juwara,

I am pleased to inform you of our plans to visit Njawara on behalf of the Manding Medical Centre. I am the advisor and instructor for a group of college students from Alpena Community College in Michigan in the USA.

We plan to visit Njawara in May and hope you will help us find lodging with local families during our stay. Our plan as of now is to fly out of the US on May 6th to Banjul via London and to return on May 19th 2005.

During our stay in Gambia, our hope is to provide any assistance we can to the community on behalf of the Manding Medical Centre. We would like to visit the school in Njawara and tutor the children and share stories and activities with them.

I also hope that we will have the opportunity to visit the important centres of the community and learn as much as we can in our short stay about the people and life in Njawara and Gambia.

I have communicated our plans with Dr. Alhasan Ceesay, who has kindly extended the invitation to us on behalf of the Manding Medical Centre.

Sincerely

Thomas P. Ray

English Instructor

This letter was acknowledged by the commissioner and the district authority in the Gambia. Now that I was certain of the trip I set to inform my board members in like manner. The certainty of the trip was concretized by the following sent by Tom on 10 March 2005.

It simply updated me on the progress made regarding the trip; that the students have raised half the money needed to travel to Gambia. He affirms the fact that everyone concerned is working hard on the remaining sum. The arranged inoculations and are preparing to apply for visas to Gambia.

He said they were all enthused and has used my address in Gambia for the visa information requirement. Again, I was delighted for things are now heading the right direction for the historic and unique trip to Njawara.

I am now certain that more doors to boost ours and the centre's goals for the Gambia will be open by this simple friendly act of ACC. Here finally is my despatch the board members of Manding Medical Centre at Njawara village.

MANDING MEDICAL CENTRE/NJAWARA

UNITED KINGDOM CONTACT

245 GREAT WESTERN STREET

MANCHESTER, M14 4LQ

ENGLAND

E-MAl:alhasanceesay@hotmail.com

Tel/Fax: 44+161-342-0854

Date: 25/03/05

DEAR BOARD MEMBER,

I am pleased to bring to your attention about American guests to Manding Medical Centre at Njawara. Mr. Thomas Ray along with 11 Alpena Community college students will be visiting the Gambia as our guest in May 2005. They will be leaving the USA for the Gambia on May 6th, 2005 and depart for United States on the 19th, of May.

I would be most grateful if you give some of your time to meet them and make their visit memorable. There are many benefits to be accrued for the centre and the Gambia. I am at present arranging in the form of scholarships or placements in various fields of study at my previous college in Alpena Michigan.

I have been in constant contact with Commissioner Batala Juwara at Kerewan and I would like all of you to brain storm and make this an ongoing link between us and Alpena Community College and other Michigan cities I am now in negotiation with. Alpena city has developed interest in our project.

I am also happy to report that my former college, Alpena Community College has awarded me, "Distinguished 2005 Graduate." Find enclosed correspondence from Mr. Thomas Ray, in behalf of the Leadership class of Alpena Community College, to Commissioner Juwara and Sefo Fafanding Kinte.

I look forward to your understanding and participation to help open up the Pandoa's Box of goodwill for the Gambia. This is a onetime opportunity for the Gambia that would make our two people linked for good goals and noble courses for generations of Gambians.

My regards and keep in touch.

Yours truly,

Dr. Alhasan S. Ceesay, MD

Founder/co-coordinator

Cc: Mr. Ousainu Darboe

Mr. Fafa E. Mbai

Dr. Dawda Ceesay

Dr. Ayo Palmer

Mr. Saim Kinte

Mr. Sambou Kinte

Mr. Mustapha Njie

Mr. Maja Sonk

Mr. Dodou Ceesay

Mr. Sisawo Ceesay

Mrs. Mbee Sonko

On April 7th 2005, Tom updated me stating that the visa applications were going well and that most of the students have received their visas. In addition let me privilege you the reader with some of the reactions emailed to me about the pending trip and what it would mean to them.

Alison Jane Smolinski said: "Hello Dr. Ceesay. I am one of the students in the Leadership class at Alpena Community College. I am really excited about the service trip, only a couple more weeks.

Right now we are trying to prepare for the trip, just getting the basic necessities and what we should be packing. I just read about how you are building a bakery at Njawara. Even though our resources are limited, is there something we could do to help out? I thought we could help in some way.

I also just wanted to say thank you for the wonderful experience you giving to us. I realize it will be truly an eye opener. I feel as if I could never be able to repay you for these two weeks that you about to give us. Thank you Dr. Ceesay!"Another email from Brittany Postumus simply stated; "I am one of the students from Alpena Community College that will be coming this May to help.

After learning all the things that you have done I must say you are an inspiration and the world can use more people who care as much as you do. I can't wait to come to Njawara. I am very excited to be able to help and thank you for the invitation."

Lastly, Ms. Grace Schimitz sent in the following before leaving for the Gambia. "I am a member of the Alpena Community College class that will be assisting you this May at Njawara. I am greatly looking forward to my visit to the Gambia.

Thank you so much for the invitation! The Friends of Manding, a charitable Trust at Colchester had the following in its web site about the trip to Njawara, the Gambia. It read as "News flash 12 American visiting:"

"A class of 11 students and their instructor Mr. Thomas Ray from Alpena Community College, Alpena Michigan, will be visiting the Gambia as guest of Manding Medical Centre from the 6th to 19th May 2005. They will be visiting communities and tutor at local schools. Alpena has developed interest in project Manding Medical Centre at Njawara.

We are negotiating to have this exchange as an ongoing affair between Alpena and Njawara." As time drew near to the flight to the Gambia Tom contacted the Commissioner on several occasions to clear last possible huddles that may surface.

None the less preparations went smoothly and Thomas Ray and his ACC Leadership class left America on May 10th 2005 via Madrid and then Dakar, Senegal before embanking at Banjul, the Gambia.

As fate would have the team instead hired a bus from Dakar to Hamdali village in the North Bank which was nearer to Njawara. I learnt they were given a VIP escort from Hamdali via Kerewan to Njawara village.

As expected, I called the Mayor of Njawara, Mrs. Hadi Panneh enquiring about the American visitors. She told me they were fine and housed at the village centre, a semi motel used for foreign guest to Njawara. Tom and I spoke at length along with Sefo Fafanding Kinte.

Sefo Fafanding reassured me that everything possible will be done to help make "our guest comfortable and likewise a memorable visit in due course. I spoke briefly to the commissioner the next day to get a feedback from him. The two week flew fast for the students most of who did want to leave at the time for kindness rendered by the villagers.

It is said that good thing never last long and this the experience of the student who went to Njawara in May 2005.Here is the reaction of Americans after the trip to the Gambia. The ACC students started sending their report and experience as guest of Manding Medical Centre, Njawara, The Gambia.

Starting with Alison Jane Smolinski reported as bellow. "Hello Dr. Ceesay: The trip to Njawara was incredible! I did not want to leave. It was an experience of a lifetime that I will never forget. Everyone in the village was very kind and helpful. I have never met such kind people in my entire life. I found the villagers doing everything possible to make their lives better.

I realized that many people work together to get a job done or finished. This is absolutely wonderful. Everyone was so helpful in the village. The people of Njawara gave us such wonderful hospitality. The food and shelter was more than we deserved.

Also your wife, Mrs Fatou Koma-Ceesay, was all too good to us. We had a remarkable time with her at Bundung/Serekunda. Her cooking was excellent. And the gifts she gave all of us, we did not deserve.

Your family is wonderful and was too kind to us.I would like to thank you for the incredible experience you have given me. I could not have asked for anything more. I immensely enjoyed myself.

I want to go back one day. I also want you to know that I will do my best to help in whatever way I can. I realize that action are louder than words and hope I can prove that to everyone. Thank you Dr. Ceesay."

Another reaction came from Grace Schiminitz. "I really enjoyed my time in Njawara. The people treated us very well and it was a pleasure to spend two weeks with them. Your wife is a wonderful person and was very hospitable to us.

I will always be grateful for her kind treatment. I hope to make another visit to Njawara in the future. It is a wonderful place. It was an eye-opening experience. The people were absolutely marvellous.

They treated us as their own family and welcomed us with open hands. I had no idea that they would be that hospitable. I really miss walking to the river and spending time with the children. It was my first experience in Gambia and hopefully it will not be my last. I hope I can return their kindness.

I would love to see how the kids have grown up."The last but not the least came from Mr. Thomas P. Ray, English instructor at ACC. It read; "I want to thank you for the opportunity you provided my students on this trip. The entire experience was enjoyable and valuable as a means of teaching my students something about the responsibility that comes with the privileges they enjoy here. Everyone was kind to us on the trip and the students came away with many great souvenirs and memories. I have many digital photos and am working on producing a CD of them to send out. I also plan to type up a version of my journal for posting on the internet and I will send parts of that to you.

I plan to call the village this weekend to extend my appreciation to everyone. Do you know anything about the proposed potential sister city relationship between Alpena and Njawara? I would like to start making some local contacts here to help that process. I am also hopeful that future trips will be possible for my students.

-Mr. Thomas P. Ray-

As you know very well man proposes but God dispose things. Tom took over the running of the department and with that came a hand full challenging responsibilities. He was not able to provide the CD until 11th of October 2005 after several reminders from me and those visiting my Website (www.friendsofmandinggambimed.btck.co.uk or www.publishkunsa.com).

Finally, Tom contacted me on 4/11/05 to let me know he had the college mailing office send the CD of photos and other material registered delivery to me. Then he made donation of $1000(one thousand us dollars) in the name of Friends of Manding, a Charitable Trust at Colchester Essex organising fund raising activities for Manding

Medical Centre at Njawara the Gambia, West Africa. This cheque was duly received and forward registered mail to the Secretary of the Friends of Manding for depositing into our account at LLyod's Bank in Colchester Essex County. Tom asked about the state of the proposed sister-city program between Alpena and Njawara.

Yes, this was one of my goals for inviting the Americans to my village in the Gambia. I just believe that unveiling the false masks and stigma others have about Africa will create harmony in its unique way.

People need to accept differences in the cultures.I transmitted all reactions presented by our American visitor to the Commissioner, the chief, and the village heads especially Hadi Panneh of Njawara village.

ALPENA: THANKS FOR TWINING WITH US/SISTER-CITY PROCLAMATION.

Having now been recognized as Distinguished 2005 Graduate by Alpena Community College I made a proposal for a twining relationship or sister-city status between Alpena and select villages in the Gambia. I, you guessed right, contacted Mathew Dunckel as a sound board or trial balloon for the above idea.

He replied that it was a sound idea and suggested my contacting the Alpena City Council members on the subject. He gave their web site thus:

http://www.alpena.mi.us/council/members. In addition
he gave the names of Councilman Dave Karschnik and
Councilwoman Carol Shafto for me to initiate direct
contact with the Alpena City Council. He told me that the
mayor was John Gilmet and the City manager was Mr.
Alan Bakalarski.

Armed with all this information and more I made my first
push through Mrs. Penny Boldrey, Executive Director at
Alpena Community College. I had no doubt if I get her
interest in this unique wish she would do all within her
power to not only contact the right people to make it
eventually happen but would open up more doors for my
villagers and our health project at Njawara.

Penny Boldrey upon hearing from me linked with
Councilwoman Shafto on the June 14th, 2005 thus; "Hi
Carol, from one Distinguished Grad to another….. I
received the enclosed message from our 2005
Distinguished Graduate, Dr. Alhasan Ceesay.

I' m wondering if perhaps you can help me with his
inquiry regarding the possibility of twining between
Alpena City and two villages in the Gambia, West Africa."
Penny in turn informed me that she had contacted a
good friend, Carol Shafto, who is a member of Alpena's
City Council and also an Alpena Community College
Distinguished 2003 Graduate, regarding my request for
twining between the above communities. She enclosed

Councilwoman Shafto's response to the idea. My reaction was swift and my message to Councilwoman Carol Shafto ran thus:-"Hello Councilwoman Carol. Mrs Penny Boldrey sent me correspondence she had with you regarding a proposal I made to the city of Alpena.

My initial e-mail kick starting a twining proposal between the city of Alpena; Njawara and Kinte Kunda villages in the Gambia West Africa was sent to Mayor John F. Gilmet, Dave R. Karsctunick, Mike Polluch, Sam Eller and Carol Shafto.

It read, "I'm pleased to write and inform you that I am deputized by village heads of Njawara and Kinte Kunda to contact you and initiate a twining/sister city status proposal between Alpena and the above two villages. Njawara is my home village and Kinte Kunda is where I attended primary school in the early fifties.

Tom Ray and the Leadership students visited both places during their two weeks stay in the Gambia. They met the chief of the district, Sefo Fafanding Kinte, at Kinte Kunda. Kinte Kunda has been the seat of many chiefs of the region and Fafanding is the most recent of several from this village.

Njawara is historically a trading centre connecting Gambia and the Northern part of Senegal. Today she has become a tourist destination. One can easily log onto information about Njawara village on the internet.

It boasts of lots of female education oriented projects. In addition it has an agricultural training centre."The contact was made in behalf of the village heads of the above and the local authority at the North Bank division of the Gambia.

This twining would be a very rewarding interaction and educational for both yours and the villagers. The people are eager to make worthwhile friendship with America. The chiefs and village heads have urged me to initiate their wish for the twining between them and Alpena or any city willing to go into such relationship with the villages.

You can link up with Mr. Thomas Ray and his students for feedback on their experience as guests of Manding Medical Centre at Njawara village, the Gambia. The villagers and I would be most grateful if given the chance to link up with Alpena City.

Carol Shafto sent in this hiccup. "Dr. Ceeasy, I cannot proceed with any more discussions with the City Council of the City of Alpena until I am much clearer about what a Twining proposal entails. Could you please describe to me what you have in mind?

Although we may be supportive of your work at Njawara and Kinte Kunda in the Gambia; we cannot really act on your request until we know what we are agreeing to. Could you send me a brief outline of what you are seeking from the City of Alpena?I will be happy to act as a liaison between you and the City, but cannot do so until I have a clear idea of what I am advocating for. Thank you most sincerely."

–Carol-

On July 13, 2005 I sent the required clarification to Councilwoman Carol Shafto as follows. Hello Carol, I am glad to hear from you. To be simplistically clear, twining means a sisterhood relationship between two cities for the mutual rewards of those involved.

 Hence it is a friendship like affair where people from Alpena can be part of and likewise the villages involved but at no cost to either party. For example Councilwoman Shafto can choose to spend two weeks in Gambia helping reorganize or create a more functional administrative system or even learn from the villagers.

In brief it is a two way international relationship. Or cultural dance -troupes from the Gambia villages can be coming to entertain Alpena, possibly more cities, during the summers. This will help raise funds for the city, the villages, like wise for our health project at Njawara.

It will provide much awareness and understanding of the two people merged in friendship. It is like adopting each other and opening up rewarding human adventures at no cost involved.

In a nut-shell, it means ratified friendship between Alpena and the two villages. I hope this makes it palatable for Alpena to want to be part of such endearing relationship. I thank you in behalf of the Kerewan local authority, the villagers and Commissioner for North Bank Division, the Gambia. God blesses all of you." –

Dr. Ceesay

Needless to say Councilwoman Carol Shafto was very pleased with the above clarification and appealed to Alpena City Council to consider the idea of twining in behalf of the Gambian villages.

Hence, Carol on the 13/7/05 sent me this e-mail following the receipt of the above message to the councilwoman. It simply states that, "I have forwarded this information to the mayor and city manager and offered to be the liaison if the City should consent to comply with this request.

I will keep you posted with any development." I updated the Commissioner and all concern at the Lower Badibou district regarding progress of my initiative with Alpena City few weeks after hearing from Councilwoman Carol Shafto. The Commissioner and the local authority sent me the bellow covering letter in support of my push for a twining relationship with Alpena City Michigan, USA.

Njawara/Kinte Kunda

Lower Badibou District

North Bank Division

The Gambia, W. Africa

E-mail:njawaranato@yahoo.co.uk

November 5th, 2005

To: Dr. Alhasan Ceesay

Manchester, England

Subject: Twining of Njawara, Kinte Kunda & Alpena Michigan

Dear Dr. Ceesay,

Your first letter dated September 23rd, 2005 has been received and the content of which is understood, both the Commissioner, the Chief and the Alkalos (village heads) of Njawara and Kinte Kunda are very much interested in having Njawara, Kinte Kunda and Alpena City twined.

The Communities of both villages met and discussed the issue and they are very much happy about the lofty ideas. Njawara and Kinte Kunda are located in the Northern part of the Gambia. They are just about 60 kilometres away from the capital City Banjul, the Gambia.

Kinte Kunda is just 2 kilometres away from our administrative headquarters Kerewan where both the Commissioner and Area Council stay. Whereas Njawara is located 9 kilometres away from Kerewan. Regards

Sincerely

Aja Hadi Panneh (Alkalo)

Alh. Fafanding Kinte (Chief Lower Badibou)

Cc: Mr. Batala Juwara (Commisioner NBD)

I replied to the above support with this note despatched immediately to the village Akalos, the Chief and Commissioner North Bank Division at Kerewan village.

245 Great Western Street

Manchester M14 4LQ

England

16/11/05

A BIG THANK YOU TO ALL

Dear Commissioner,

I'm profoundly grateful to you, Sefo Fafanding, the local authority (area Council and chiefs) and especially Alkalo Arfang Bah and people of Toro. Lastly but not the least a big thank you goes to the people of Badibou, Njawara and my sister Hadi Panneh Alkalo of Njawara village. I am very happy for support and understanding given to

Manding Medical Centre. I'm pleased to inform you that I have initiated a twining process between Alpena and the villages of Njawara and Kinte Kunda. I have forwarded your note of 5/11/05 to the Alpena City Council. Copies were also sent to Mr. Thom Ray and the college.

Again, thank you for making our American friends happy and welcomed to our beloved country. God bless all of you. I will continue working for our development.

Sincerely

Dr. Alhasan S. Ceesay, MD

Director/Founder

Manding Medical Centre.

I then sent Carol Shafto the letter from the district authority plus this note urging action from her end.

245 Great Western Street

Manchester M14 4LQ

 England

8/11/05

Mrs. Carol Shafto

Councilwoman

Alpena City Council

208 North First Avenue

Alpena, MI 49707

Dear Mrs. Carol Shafto,

The enclosed is reply to your last e-mail dated 25/9/05 regarding the twining proposal made to the Alpena City Council earlier on by me in behalf of Njawara village and Kinte Kunda, the Gambia, respectively.

The enthusiasm about having this relationship with Alpena is immeasurable. The villagers are looking forward to a warm and fruitful relationship between the two people. They all pray that you would be as eager to consummate it as they have already done in their wishes and hearts.

Finally, may friendship and human kindness be an everlasting link between all humans. God bless you and we look forward for a positive reply soon.

My personal regards and thanks to the City Council and all of Alpena.

Yours Sincerely

Dr. Alhasan S. Ceesay, MD

It was not until September21, 2005 that I sent Councilwoman Shafto the following reminder and follow up note. "Hi Carol, I hope you had an enjoyable summer. This is a follow up of that lofty idea of twining Alpena City with Njawara and Kinte Kunda villages in the Gambia. Has there been any movement forward at the Mayor's Office about the proposal made to the city? Is there anything I or the district authority in Gambia need do to bring this to fruition?

I have not heard anything about it since your last email of 14/7/05. Again, regards and thanks. I bank on your continued interest. God Bless."

–Dr. Ceesay-

The next day God smiled onto our dream to befriend America. Councilwoman Mrs. Carol Shafto sent me the following reply to the inquiry about the status of my dream for America and the Gambia.

It rang in the most melodious and cherished message I ever had for a long, long time after my being admitted into medical school and upon treating my first patient in the villages. Here is Carol's email to me. "Good morning Dr. Ceesay: I appreciate your persistence in accomplishing this goal. Without that it surely would have failed. I do apologize for this delay. I have just returned this week from a wonderful month long tour of the UK and Ireland.

My last communication, before I left, with the City Manager was that this was a good idea, will be good for public relations, and that we should go forward with the proposal. The Mayor is also in favour. So there is absolutely nothing standing in the way of this happening. I am willing to do the work of it, but I honestly have no idea what to do.

Do you know procedures or paper work or any such thing from your end? Is it as simple as a proclamation? I would like to have more information about your village, your people, and why you are interested in twining with Alpena – what connection there is.

I would then put together a presentation for the City Council and ask them to decide that we are sister-cities (the term used here, although I know the UK and Europe use "twining) with the villages of Njawara and Kinte Kunda.

We could erect a sign at the City entrance, etc. If you have any idea or directions for me, please let me know. Also any information you can provide on your village would be helpful. I will continue to work with you on this until it is accomplished.

Your friend in Alpena – Carol Shafto –

This was followed by my forwarding the bellow addendum to whatever had reached the Councilwoman's desk. Being the architect of this union much was expected from me. And so I never relented supplying as much information as many times as I can afford.

My phone bill sprouted to a Warping £600 etc. Most important was this addendum bellow.

SYNAPSIES OF NJAWARA/KINTE KUNDA VILLAGES

Njawara is a 350 years old market village situated on the bank of the Miniminiyang bolong, a creek of the River Gambia, in the Lower Badibou District of the North Bank Division of the Gambia. Njawara has a population of a thousand residents and is 95 kilometres from Banjul, Gambia's capital City.

The village lies close to the Senegalese border and has been the trade links between Gambia and Senegal during the colonial days. Njawara was established and founded by the Panneh family of the Wolof tribe and initially called "Panneh village". The elderly still fondly refer to her as Mpanneh.

Among the residents of now Njawara are Mandingkas, Fulas, Sereres, Jolas, Konyanginkas, and Mabara tribes. All of whom are farmers, with few serving as petty traders, growing Peanuts, Rice, Coos, and a variety of vegetables.

The nearest government administrative post is 9 kilometres away at Kerewan village. Njawara lacked modern luxuries of electricity, proper telephones, sewer system, pave roads but water is now pumped from a nearby borehole.

The village has a thriving school and a dynamic citizenry working hard to improve their lot and the future of the younger generation.

KINTE KUNDA village has been the political base of Lower Badibou District for decades. It has provided us with several chiefs in the past and Sefo Fafanding Kinte is the most recent contribution. Kinte Kunda village comprises of mostly Mandinka tribes men and women.

It is the home of venerable late Sefo Njako Kinte who, in the 30s ruled the district with an iron fist. It was he who imposed one of his brothers, Almami Kinte, to take over the administration or village headship of then Njawara(Mpanneh). None the less he was a respected chief.

Kinte Kunda was the first village that had a school in the entire Lower Badibou district and I am told that he chief insisted that the school be built in his home village leaving a row that lasted through his rein.

The village is now a smaller population than Njawara and the current appointed chief of the district, Sefo Fafanding Kinte resides there. Residents of Kinte Kunda are all farmers eager to improve their lives and those of their children.

They are friendly, peaceful, charming, descent hard working people who contributed a lot to growth of the

Lower Badibou District in the North Bank. These two villages along with the entire Lower Badibou District yearn for this twining/sister-city status to come to realty. Hence, I enclose relevant messages regarding the proposed twining from the district authority as per fax from the Gambia.

The villagers and I are interested in twining with Alpena Michigan n an effort to open up the Pandora's box of friendship, goodwill and more understanding of the people and cultures that would allow us relate in this shrinking globe we all share. There is a lot we can do for each other once the ugly veil of ignorance, misunderstanding and fear is removed.

And this can be done only learning and interacting with one another. I am sure the students, who went to the villages, can tell how much warmth and friendship they received from the villagers they met. Exchange visits and whole host of beneficial programs to both parties can be organized within the framework of this twining.

Once again, I personally appeal to the Mayor and City Council of Alpena to give this desire of the villagers a chance of fruition for Alpena City and the above villages in the Gambia.

BY: DR. ALHASAN SISAWO CEESAY, MD

In short while, I received the following reply from Councilwoman Carol Shafto of Alpena City Council letting me know of the final details, date of the be proclamation for the sister-city relationship between our villages and Alpena Michigan. Without further ado I present the message as sent on the 17th of November 2005.

"Good Morning Dr. Ceesay

After many months of communication with you, I can finally announce a DATE for our Twining/Sister City Resolution! The Alpena City Council will adopt a resolution to establish a Sister City Program with Njawara/ Kinte Kinda on December 5th, 2005.

I am going to be personally preparing the resolution. Since it will be a part of permanent records for both the villages and the City of Alpena, I would like be sure all of the information is accurate. Penny Boldrey suggested that I email the text to you after I complete it.

If you are willing, you could read it for any factual errors or omissions before I send it on to the City. If you are willing, I will send that via email when it is ready, sometime next week.

Meanwhile I am meeting with Tom Ray from the college who led the Leadership Class expedition to the villages. He is VERY enthusiastic about this proposal and is going to give me information and even share some pictures.

We will be meeting next week. Finally, I have invited several people to come to the City Council meeting to provide testimony and support for this proposal. Both Penny Boldrey and Tom Ray will be there.

Also they are inviting some of the students who went to the villages to also be present and speak to the issue. So it would be a very nice presentation and will be more than just a formality.

Also, if you would like, I can arrange to have a tape of the meeting sent to you. Our meetings are videotaped and played for the public on the public access television channel several times a week, between meetings. I can make a copy of the tape of the meeting and have it send you or to the village officials or both if you would like.

Also, the resolution will have an official seal of the City of Alpena and the signature of the Mayor. I will have as many copies as you need made and will laminate them so they will be preserved. I will send those to you and/ or whomever you designate. I will get several if necessary.

I am so pleased to finally be able to bring this to completion. I know it must have been frustrating to you to have this take so long and to have us seen to be so unresponsive. I hope this totally enthusiastic ending makes up for all of that! Your friend in Alpena: -

Carol Shafto

On the day of ratification or passing of the resolution for sister city relationship between Alpena and the two above villages several speakers were heard. These included, among many, Penny Bodrey, Mr. Tom Ray, two student representatives who visited Gambia in May 2005 and Dr. Avery Aten.

This was buffered by loop of fifty photos of the villages taken by the student while in the Gambia. At the end of the presentation Mayor John F. gimlet read into the record the above proclamation and vote was tabled to pass it.

This Sister City proclamation between Alpena with Njawara/Kinte Kunda, Lower Badibou District, the Gambia was moved by Councilwoman Carol Shafto, seconded by Councilman Karschnick, that the proclamation to establish a sister city program with the villages of Njwara and Kinte Kunda be approved. The move was carried by unanimous vote.

A copy of the sister City Resolution passed by Alpena City Council on December 5th 2005 is reproduced for your pleasure to read.

Chapter 22

PROCLAMATION TO ESTABLISH A "SISTER CITY" PROGRAM WITH
NJAWARA AND KINTE KUNDA, LWER BADIBOU DISTRICT, GAMBIA, WEST
AFRICA

WHEREAS, the City of Alpena recognizes and supports the concept of global cooperation and community; and

WHERAS, the villagers of Njawara and Kinte Kunda, through their local leaders and Dr. Alhasan S. Ceesay, have reached out their hand in friendship and goodwill, and

WHEREAS, relationships were established by students and faculty of Alpena Community College when they were warmly welcomed to the villages for a service project earlier this year, and

WHEREAS, mutual understanding of our diversities as well as our similarities and the cultural exchanges that will result, will be beneficial to the citizens of both areas, and

WHEREAS, true global community is often established one person at a time, and one city and village at a time, leading to beneficial relations and programs for all;

NOW, THEREFORE, I, John F. Gilmet, by virtue of the authority vested in me as Mayor, DO HEREBY PROCLAIM, a "Sister City" Program with the villages of

NJAWARA/KINTE KUNDA

LOWER BADIBOU DISTRICT

GAMBIA

And urge all area citizens to extend the hand of fellowship and an embrace of genuine fraternity to their friends in NJAWARA/KINTE KINTE KUNDA and pledge support and loyalty as these communities of two great nations join together as "Sister Cities"

Signed at Alpena Michigan, United States of America, on this 5th day of December, 2005. Councilwoman Carol Shafto read the following reply from me to Council and residents of Alpena City.

ALPENA, THANKS FOR TWINING WITH US

Honourable Mayor John F. Gilmet, Alpena City Council and residents of Alpena; please allow me convey heartfelt thanks as well as greetings from the Commissioner, NBD, Kerewan Area Council, the Chief of Lower Badibou, the Alkalos (village heads) of Njawara and Kinte Kunda. I am today full of joy and gratitude for twining resolution ratified by the Alpena City Council.

I am speechless as one of my dreams for the villager and America has now materialized in this twining resolution passed by Alpena. We are two good people now merged in good will for humanity and friendship. This coming together will archive a lot for both of us. There is a lot for us to gain as well as learn from each other and generations to come will thank us for having taken the first footsteps of bringing people of diverse cultures and understanding together.

Enclosed is message from the Gambia in response to the most welcomed news in your last email. This is the top of the iceberg for there is lot more benefit in this act. In addition, as long as I am alive Alpena and Gambia will not only benefit from this unique venture but will smile yearly for having dreamt along with me.

 Let me, in passing, mention with thanks the first harbingers of this day. They are Mr. Thomas P. Ray and his Leadership team of students from Alpena Community College who visited Njawara village in May 2005. Thomas Ray and the students laid the marvellous foundation we today concretize.

Mrs. Penny Boldrey and Mathew Dunckel deserve our appreciation for remaining interested and in constant contact with me. The Gambia, the district authority of Lower Badibou and villagers remain eternally grateful for giving us the chance of twining with you.

A Huge thanks Alpena City, the Mayor of Alpena and Alpena City Council for work well done. Councilwoman Mrs. Carol Shafto who relentlessly steered the twining proposal to completion also deserves our profound gratitude. The villagers and I are eternally indebted to all at Alpena. In addition, we look forward to working hand in hand for the reward of all parties.

Finally, I would again like to pay tribute to past and present friends at Alpena who helped me reach this pedestal. All of you helped make my sojourn to America a remarkable success. I would like many more of my friends to be like you at Alpena. I hope you will believe, as well as join me, in my dream of providing modern medical aid to the Gambian villagers. Thanks a million and God bless America!

Signed: DR. ALHASAN SISAWO CEESAY, MD

FOUNDER/COORDINATOR

MANDING MEDICAL CENTRE

NJAWARA, THE GAMBIA

Two weeks later I received three copies of the "sister City Proclamation" along with a video tape of the Alpena City Council Meeting of December 5, 2005. Also enclosed were the Alpena news and copy of Alpena Public Notices showing minutes of the City Council meeting which carried ratification of the sister city proclamation by a unanimous vote.

I must confess exhilaration in my heart for Alpena City Council having done so much for my villages without reservation and accomplished with great speed. I sent the following communiqué to the current representative to the Gambia, Ambassador Joseph D. Stafford in preparing them for the arrival the package from the Alpena City Council for forwarding to the Commissioner of the North Bank Division, the Gambia.

MANDING MEDICAL CENTRE

245 Great Western Street

Manchester M14 4LQ
Email:alhasanceesay@hotmail.com

Date: 10/12/05

Ambassador Joseph D. Stafford

Embassy of the United States of America

Kairaba Avenue

P. M. Box 19

Banjul, the Gambia,

West Africa

RE: Manding Medical Centre/Alpena USA Twining

Dear Ambassador Stafford,

I am Dr. Alhasan S. Ceesay from Njawara village and currently on studies in the UK. This is to introduce the above self-help health organisation at Njawara as well as kindly request favour of your good office's service in behalf Alpena Michigan and the villages of Njawara and Kinte Kunda, the Gambia.

I pioneered the above centre, after graduating as a doctor and upon returning to the Gambia in 1992. It became an NGO in 1994 after being fully registered by the Justice Department and recognised by the Ministry of Health in 1993. In addition, we are now a registered Charitable Trust, as Friends of Manding, in England and Wales by the Charity Commission of the UK.

Our website is: beehive thisisessex gambimed. It will show our home page as "Friends of Manding." Alternatively, one can used a short cut by typing in "Manding Medical Centre, Njawara" and click search. The same home page plus lot more will appear.

I have also written two books and a hefty portion of proceed from the sale of both books is earmarked to help support Manding Medical Centre at Njawara and our goal of providing medical aid to the villager, especially children.

More information about my work and commitment to providing much needed medical service to the region in conjunction with the Gambia Ministry of Health can be seen in our website as above. Finally, I am more than delighted to report that Alpena City, Michigan, USA has just ratified a sister city program with my home village Njawara and Kinte Kunda village in the Lower Badibou District, North Bank Division, the Gambia.

Hence, I have asked the Alpena City Mayor's Office to send five copies of the final proclamation declaring the sister city status between Alpena and the above two named villages in Badibou to you for your office to kindly deliver the documents to the Commissioner North Bank Division at Kerewan.

Thank you for taking time to assist us in the above matter. Please feel free to contact me any time convenient to you. Best wishes for good health and achievement in the coming year. Regard to your family.

Yours Sincerely

Dr. Alhasan S. Ceesay, MD

Founder/Coordinator

Manding Medical Centre

Njawara, The Gambia, West Africa.

This letter was followed with two telephone calls to the Embassy of the United States in the Gambia to verify receipt of the package sent from Alpena to Joseph D. Stafford.

The Secretary to Mr. Stafford, in the last phone call let me know it usually take a month or more before none official mail arrives at their desk. He assured me that the office will do as request whenever the package reaches the Embassy.

I called Sefo Fafanding Kinte and Alkalo Hadi Panneh and told them to check with either Ambassador Joseph Stafford directly or one of the officers in the know at the office for their copies of the sister city proclamation of which the villagers are unsung heroes for having received the ACC students who visited Njawara in May 2005 with open hearts, hospitality, generosity and warmth.

It was not until Thursday, February 16th, 2006 that Ambassador Joseph D. Stafford and team where able to deliver, in person amid tumultuous reception and celebration, the sister-city proclamation between Alpena City, Michigan USA, with Njawara and Kinte Kunda villages in the North Bank of the Gambia.

I made it clear that the brief ceremony at Njawara on the 16/2/06 marked the end of phase one of the sister city relationship between us and Alpena Michigan. I suggested the following four areas for food for thought by all concern. They are:-

Education

This already started in earnest as some in Alpena have expressed desire to sponsor worthy candidates at the primary level for an experimental period of one year. Higher levels, such as college education and nursing training and or other relevant skill areas will in due course be included.

1. Health

A lot is planned for health oriented programs and Manding Medical Centre will be enhanced to a much functional status. There will be training programs for health personnel etc.

3. Tourism: I am studying ways of creating tourist attraction with facilities erected in due course to the region.

4. Cultural: Exchanges entailing having cultural dance troop(s) from the Lower Badibou District travel to Alpena Michigan, and other cities in the USA during the summers to display our fabric of entertainment, history and arts.

These are few ideas in the pipeline. Feel free to add yours to enrich the program. This is by no means binding or final but seeking more suggestions on how to benefit both parties in this unique twining program just approved by Alpena City. Let me make it crystal clear that there is no financial commitment from Alpena.

However, the cultural show can raise lot of money upon performing in America. I thanked the Commissioner North Bank, Sefo of Lower Badibou, District Authority and Kerewan Area Council for having worked so hard with me to provide this excellent opportunity to our people. I promised that more is on the way.

Three weeks earlier I received this e-mail from Councilwoman Mrs. Carol Shafto announcing the good news of her efforts. "Dr. Ceesay, we have sent five copies of the proclamation to the America Embassy- which you provided the address for.

I also have three copies of the proclamation for you as well as a copy of the tape of the meeting; a copy of the newspaper where the action appeared; and a copy of the newspaper with the official minutes. I will get these out to you today. It was a most wonderful evening as you will see on the tape. Five people, your friends old and new, spoke in favour of the proclamation.

This included Dr. Avery Aten who I have now spoken with and who is very enthusiastic about working on the medical aspect of things with you. He will be in touch with you by phone he said. But you will be able to see him and hear what he had to say during City Council meeting of December 5, 2005.

Also speaking where two students who have visited the Gambia; Tom Ray and Penny Boldrey. (And me, of course). I read your wonderful letter for the record. We also had a loop of over fifty slides showing on the screen during the presentation. It was the nicest sister-city ceremony we have ever had-by far! Usually we just read the proclamation and that is it.

I think this ends my part in all of this-except for one thing. My sons and I were going to "adopt" a family through Save the Children. This involves sending a letter each month and with an amount of money. We would be happy to adopt some children from your village instead if there is an easy way to do this.

We would need a name and address and what form we could make our donation in (money order?). We are not really wealthy- but could send $20 -$25 a month for at least a year to a deserving child. Of course; we would hope that they might send a note now and then... but this all up to you.

I hope you are pleased with all that has happened.

I remained your friend.

Carol Shafto.

In reply I sent my friend Carol Shafto the following.Hello Carol; Now I am able to response to your email. First, please accept our eternal ineptness' for having worked so hard to bring the twining into reality. Only God can reward your efforts.

Please kindly extend our heartfelt gratitude to the Mayor and your fellow Counselors at Alpena. Send me the Mayor's telephone. I need to convey our appreciation to him. I had a long chat with the village and they were in cloud nine about the approval of the sister city program.

 I will be forwarding the names of deserving school children you might want to sponsor/adopt. I will cal you, before forwarding the names, about it when I get the list that the parents and headmaster promised to send me. Thanks a million and God blesses you and yours. Best wishes for good health and successful 2006. I look forward to our travelling to the Gambia soon. Regard.

Sincerely

Dr. Alhasan S. Ceesay, MD

In the mean time Mrs. Penny Boldrey was also busy doing a story for the ACC Alumni News. In addition Carol was able to have a feature about the just approved sister city program done by the local news paper. She was very happy about it as the email bellow from Carol shows.

"Good Morning Alhasan, "our story" is headline, above the fold, in the Alpena News today! It is wonderful publication for your project. I will send you copies but you can read it on-line today only at www.thealpenanews.com. It reads "Alpena's sister-city-ACC graduate initiates partnership with Gambia villages."

And there is a wonderful colour picture of one of the ACC students with village children. I hope you enjoyed the story and are pleased with my efforts for publicity. The news reporter, Sue Lutuszek, will do a follow-up story about people "adopting Children for education purposes", like I am doing with my son(s).

It is a good day for celebration. Check the website.

Your friend

Carol

Here is one of several features about the twining between Alpena City with Njwara and Kinte Kunda villages in the North Bank Division, the Gambia.

ALPENA NEWS MICHIGAN, USA

SISTER CITY PROGRAM HAS TIES TO

ACC STUDENT OF 1960s

A link dating back to the 1960s has helped Alpena establish a sister city program with Njawara and Kinte Kunda, Lower Badibou District, the Gambia.

The program was initiated by Alhasan Ceesay, MD, an Alpena Community College of the 1960s and the 2005 Distinguished Graduate who lives in the Wes African country. He was assisted by ACC staff and Councilwoman

Carol Shafto.

"He feels this is his American home and villages in Gambia are his African home and wanted to link the tow together." Carol Shafto said. When Penny Boldrey of the ACC Foundation first put Ceesay in touch with Shafto for assistance in the venture, Shafto was leery of his intentions.

"I did not get it," she said. "I wanted to know what we are going to gain?" the whole idea is simply to put out information on the situation in those villages in the public eye, Shafto said Ceesay's dream is to build a medical centre to serve the villages, since care is many miles away and roads in and out of villages aren't passable by ambulance.

Currently patients are transported out of villages without ambulances for distances to health centres from their homes. Avery Aten, MD, of Alpena also has become involved with the project. "The medical aspects of this relationship can be long-term," he told city council members. He said so medical statistics regarding the area, such as the average life expectancy is 53 years old and 85 out of 1000 children die during birth.

According to Shafto, some of Aten's hopes include sending medical equipment which is no longer used here to the villages and even possibly having nursing students experiencing practicing there. I just see all kinds of goodwill things happening,"

Shafto said, "For us to have the opportunity to lead about a totally different culture is good for us."

"One aspect Shafto highlighted is the opportunity for elementary classroom in Alpena to communicate with the village school. Although she assisted in having the proclamation made, Shafto gives credit for making it happen to individuals at ACC. "My part is minor compared to what ACC has done," she said. "They are the ones who really got this started."

During the trip the students met with various village leaders who showed them what projects they were working on and where the greatest need was. In addition, the students taught some short classes on the United States. One day the group helped with the construction of a mosque. They also visited the agricultural centre and health centre.

Ray said the trip "contributed greatly" in making the sister city proclamation a reality "because it gave people in Alpena a connection to the village." "The Gambia District Authority of Lower Badibou and villagers remain eternally grateful for giving us chance of twining with you.

Huge thanks to the City of Alpena, Mayor of Alpena and Alpena City Council," Alhasan wrote. "The villagers and I are enternaly indebted to all at Alpena.

In addition, we look forward to working hand in hand for reward of all parties." -Sue Latuszek: The Alpena News 2005-

The first hatchling of this merging of diverse hearts is as follows:-

Njawara Basic School

Lower Badibu District

North Bank Division

The Gambia, W. Africa

19/01/06

Dear Sir/Madam

RE: To whom it may concern.

These students are promising students whose parents are not able to fully support their educational needs. As a result, we would be very grateful if a concern person(s) can assist the students and their parents in taking care of some of the financial difficulties they are encountering to earn education.

These include school fees, uniforms, book bills and other school needs. Thank you and in anticipation, I remain,

Yours Faithfully

Lamin K. Juwara/Principal

These where the initial list of needy students who would have benefited from the Manding Medical Centre/USA scholarship grants.

NAME ADDRESS	AGE	CLASS	PARENT
1. Ismaila Ceesay Njawara	14yrs	8B	Dodu Ceesay
2. Edrisa Barry Njawara	14yrs	8B	Adoulie Barry
3. Alieu Dem Njawara	12yrs	7B	Modou Dem
4. Mamud Panneh Njawara	12yrs	7A	Ousainu Panneh
5. Adama Jallow Ardo	12yrs	7B	Assan Jallow Ker
6. Kally Bah Ardo	13yrs	8B	Saikou Bah Ker
7. Njammeh Bah Bah	12yrs	7B	Musa Bah Toro
8. Hammed Dem Bah	12yrs	7B	Musa I. Bah Toro
9. Ebrima Kanteh Bah	15yrs	7B	Baboucar Kaneh Toro

10. Mustapha Jawo   15yrs   8A   Omar Jawo   Toro Bah

11. Modou Touray   11yrs   6A Sohna Jaw   Panneh Bah

12. Nuha Krubally 10yrs   5A   Modo Krubally   Samba Musu

13. Matarr Panneh   10yrs   4B   Bora Panneh Njawara

14. Modou Loum   14yrs   7B   Bintou Jammeh   Ker Jebal

The above list and letter were faxed to Councilwoman Carol Shafto on the 23/02/06. The fax simply read:-

Hi Carol, I hope you are okay and back at work. I hereby forward a list of school children from Njawara school needing sponsorship. Feel free to contact those you think would like to participate in this educational project. The first three candidates in the list are earmarked for you and your son(s). See names 1 – 3 in the list.

Send all monies via Western Union in the name of Aja Hadi Panneh, (Alkalo of Njawara village) to any Gambian Bank that Western Union deals with in Gambia.

Then email me stating amounts, date sent and for who. I will follow up by contacting the Principal of Njawara School, the parents and the chief of the district to ascertain prompt and proper distribution. In addition, I will have Aja Hadi Panneh (Alkalo), the parents, Headmaster and were possible the recipient students to write acknowledging the amounts received.

Please feel free to contact me if you have any questions or ideas to promote the above noble educational commitment. Once again, thanks and we remain grateful for your stand.

Your Friend

Dr. Alhasan S. Ceesay, MD

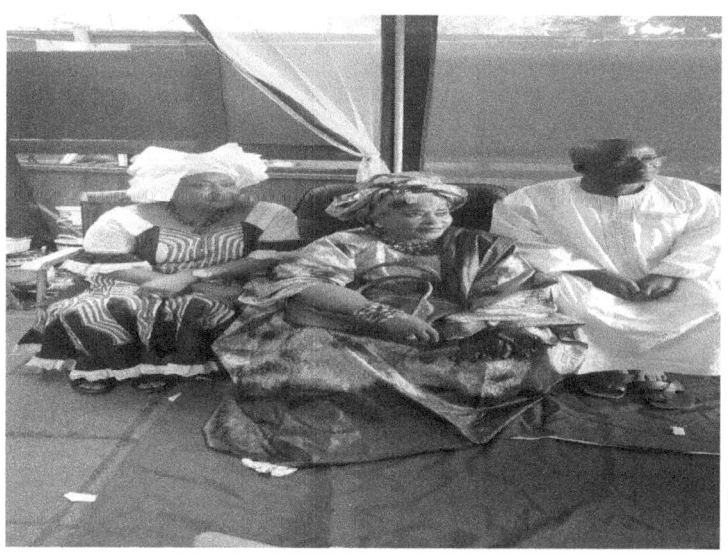

L-R: Sali Dabo, Sukai Bouvier and Kebba Dampha

Londong 2017

Chapter 23

THE WAY OF A DREAMER

Back in the Gambia a friend decried my efforts as nothing but a dream that I persistently chased. I let such observers know that it only takes time before my dream become fruitful. Here are a few examples: I left the Gambia in 1967 as a nurse and returned; after insurmountable roadblocks as a medical doctor.

While practicing in the Gambia I further created two worthy entities, namely (1) The Gambia Health Credit Union, which today provides needed financial assistance to all health workers i.e. Nurses and Health Inspectors country wide. (2) In addition I created NGO Manding Medical Centre at Njawara village, Lower Badibou to help provide a much needed medical aid and service free of charge to villagers who could not afford to pay private clinics.

With the help of visiting doctors the centre has treated more than 9000 villagers free of charge since its inception in 1993. On returning to the UK, I again with help of resident nurses and doctors in Colchester Essex setup the Friends of Manding Charitable trust in Colchester UK. This was recognized and registered as a charity in England and Wales by the UK- charity Commission in 2002.

In the midst of which I published my first book 'The Legend Against all Odds' and now has published more than thirty eight novels. To further cement my goal for the villager I was able to convince the Alpena City Council to form a sister city link with Njawara and Kinte Kunda villages in the Lower Badibous of the Gambia in 2005. This was made easier after my being awarded on May 5th, 2005 'Distinguished Graduate Award' by Alpena Community College. My web site: friends of Manding gambimed continues to lure people to Njawara to see what help they could give the villager.

Today, I am not only an author of several books; Google search: Dr. Alhasan Ceesay/books to view of purchase as contribution to rural healthcare; portions or sales from these books go to support goals of Manding medical Centre at Njawara. I am indeed a dreamer and will continue to dream fir my people. If the above is dream then here is another step to help see through me.

I am humble to let you know I am now a Publisher and my company in the UK is 'PUBLISH KUNSA LTD' and one can have their work published by logging on to our web site; www.publishkunsa.com. Again two pounds sterling from any book published by my company goes towards scholarships and rural healthcare as stipulated in terms of contract we would work on manuscripts. Dreams must be activated and not wasted.

I cannot fly without wing but can make artificial wings to let reach higher hits that loafers never can dream of. Allow the dream to force you into action. Yes, I too have a dream, which is simply that every hamlet in the Gambia be bequeathed good healthcare, safe drinking water, enough food and chance to a solid education for every child.

Yes. Education is power and a mover. I sacrificed my life to endure depravity, humiliation and solitude in other to bring medical aid to villagers. With all these I am busy trying to get more medical skills and experience before heading to Gambia, home , sweet home. With this tit-bit I can freely and willingly encourage you to dream but not to let it remain at that.

A life with trials or challenge is like an orchestra without conductor and it very defeating if not boring indeed. One must act for the good of self and any community we find ourselves. An old village sage once advice that 'A good person and at best a leader never yield to failure but only learns from it to move forward.

Grand Pa Bajoja Ceesay told me that; "One willing to do good should not expect people to remove obstacles or stones from their path; but such leaders must accept it calmly in the event these place more boulders on our way." This is what a dream turns out. At first it becomes a lonely avenue full of heartaches, which eases gradually as the good things unfold from one's relentless efforts to make the dream becomes fruitful and rewarding..

Simplly its life 99.9% very hard work full of stumbling. Do not we all dream of going to heaven? Well the path to such respites need challenging theological and spiritual discipline. Hence we earthly dreamers dabble with ideas of landing on Mars and eventually colonizing it. So allow me ask, what is your dream for mankind, especially Africa?

Can Africa ever be free of ignorance, self subtenant, corruption and misuse of the tribe? These just few multipronged toxic dragon heads African must dream to remove from our midst. With better education and discipline Africa can overcome and progress. Dreamers are doing utmost to slay the pestilent dragon hindering life in the villages of rural Africa.

We must remove the monster of retro ration for the sake of the future generation. Again grandpa Bajoja Ceesay advices that we stay the good cause and never be taken by detractions. I am no millionaire but have a million dreams worthy of pursuing for my people. Would you dream along with me? Glad to let you know hard work yields rewarding fruits.

Dream and be in control of not only your own life but be a source of hope and inspiration while contributing positively to your community. Do not be carried along by current get rich quick and live selfishly. Life is to be shared even with dreamers. Time is not mine and life will continue for the villager. Success comes slowly and brings with it contagious hope that serves as blue print for other.

The fate of mankind is up to each of us. Do not succumb to idleness. Use youthful opportunity to develop out of ignorance, and corruption by having courage to bring change to the people. Be the change you want in others. Expect resistance on your path to bring change. A useful proxy in fulfilling a dream is not letting it wane away.

Always think it possible and work hard at its realization. Be warned to think what could be done and not that which cannot be archived. Matrix of success lies in hard work with guided ski full knowledge. I will work on my dream and morrow will be my judge along with benefits accrued from it. I hope my last footprints of my journey on earth will inspire people towards doing well and sharing their worth with others. From one villager to another may this wish be true for rural Gambia.

Ahamed and Mrs. Giteh in Canada 2017

Chapter 24

CREATION OF MANDING MEDICAL CENTRE,

NJAWARA, NBR, THE GAMBIA

When God wants to destroy someone, He first made him an unusual dreamer. So Gandhi had his dream of people solving social deference none violently and Rev. Martin Luther king, jr. held onto his admirable dream of children of Jews and Gentile, black and whites holding hands and living in harmony spearheading peaceful cause for mankind.

There are the Albert Schweitzer's and mother Theresa's of the world dreamers who spent their lives believing in their dreams for mankind. My dream, since 1956, was the simple goal of providing medical aid to those far and in remote villages. The villager, who is forced to walk miles on end to seek medical aid for his already dying child, wife or friend, deserves a better health system.

Something I saw in 1956 left an indelible mark in my mind and I have since then asked and prayed that God help me bring part if not full solution to the kind of tragedy that was passing right before me. I was hopelessly unable to give relief except to comfort those involved.

In 1956, while on my way to Saba village, I met an anxious father carrying his son and his almost dead pregnant wife on the back of donkey heading for the health center at Kerewan village, another three or more miles from where I met him.

The child was vomiting yellow stuff, he was sweaty, his eyes were reverted backwards and the pregnant lady groaning every time the mule moves. There was some greenish fluid dripping off her lapper. She could barely hold the ropes controlling the donkey.

I went to Kerewan later that evening and asked about the status of that family, only to be told that the boy passed away half a mile to the dispensary and the lady was referred to the central hospital in Banjul but the family had no money to pay for her transportation nor was the River ambulance available as it was undergoing maintenance at the Dockyard.

To cut a long story short, both child and mother died because of lack of medical facilities or modern medical aid to the villager. One or all of those lives could have been saved and remain beneficial to the country than the fate that befell them.

I prayed and grieved with the family for months and redoubled my efforts at school in other to solve such development in future.

I committed myself to medicine from that day on and never regretted making such a challenging decision in my life. Hence, when on the day I was taking the Hippocratic Oath, I not only swore to uphold all therein but to make sure that God helped me not to ever deviate from my commitment and promise to be part of the solution in the health services of the Gambia.

I fervently prayed to be able to enhance health education in the villages, and for Mandinf Medical Centre to complement the existing medical facilities in the Gambia as well as ease the shortage of medical service personnel. To many, except the dreamer, such Erewhons leads to failure as they turn to be white elephants.

Some friends tease me by flatly promising to rise from their graves on the opening day of such an Alice in wonderland project. Let me make it crystal clear that I had no illusions about what was needed, or to be done and that the building of the hospital would indeed be a lifetime challenge I am fully ready to grapple with.

There would be a lot of well-wishers but very few will ever want to join until the opening day ceremonies. So first things first, I met an attorney friend Mr. Ousainou Darboe, a villager like me, on September 24, 1992, and pleaded for his assistance with the legal aspects of setting up a charitable foundation, Manding Medical center at Njawara village in the provinces for the sole purpose of providing much needed medical aid to the villager. He was very obliging and requested no payment in return for his services. In the mean time I got a board of governors elected while he prepared the memorandum and articles of association of Manding Medical Centre at Njawara village.

Also, I met with the Lower Badibou district chief, Kitabou Singateh, who by the way was my primary school class mate at Kinte Kunda from 1953 to 1957, the District Authority, Commissioner and the kerewan Area Council.

All of whom were more than delighted and did all they could under the law to help me set up a grassroots local advisory committee, which was headed by the commissioner, to assist the board and also let the villagers feel being part of the ongoing project.

At my home village, Njawara, a group organized itself and formed a pioneering committee to formally ask the Alkalo (village head/mayor) and the people of Toro Bahen village to donate the earmarked land between it and Njawara for the sole purpose of establishing the Manding Medical Centre on it.

The land issue was partially cleared by the first week of the appeal. In October 1992, Alkalo Omar Koi Bah of Toro Bahen, along with alhaj Musa (Njabi) Bah and Sirimang Bah called my brother, Doudu Ceesay, the elders of Toro Bahen and I to officially inform us that the earmarked land of two plots have been donated to me for the sole purpose of erecting a medical center and hospital facility for the villagers of the region and Gambia. We thanked him for his foresight and kindness towards future generations.

I went back to my lawyer, Ousainu Darbor who by then had finished all work needed for the registration of Manding Medical Centre. We are forever indebted to Alkalos Omar Koi, Arfang Bah, Musa (Njambi) Bah and resident Sirimang Bah, and the people of Toro village. Lastly but not the least our venerable able lawyer Mr. Ousainou Darboe, without whose kindness and legal mind the registration of Manding Medical Centre would have taken longer that it did assisted me.

I also express profound gratitude to the Hon. Chief of Lower Badibou district, Kitabou Singateh, the commissioner, and the local district authority for their understanding and willingness to contribute positively towards our goal and growth.

I submitted the registration application material to the Attorney General's Chambers at the Justice Department, Banjul, on October 22, 1992 and Manding Medical Centre was officially registered as an incorporated charitable organization under the companies Act, 1959 by the 27th of October 1992. Manding Medical Centre' certificate of incorporation is number: 224/1992.

With the completion of the paper work and registration of the center, I embarked on a blitz of letter writing informing philanthropists and organizations worldwide about Manding Medical Centre and the need for assistance or donations of medications, equipments, medical videos with which to teach our cadre and villagers to become health worker or evangelist, or nurses and to help us build the center.

To complete the establishment process, after the land was officially ours, I wrote to the following letter to the Ministry of Health informing them of the formation of Manding Medical Centre, a self –help health organization at Njawara, Lower Badibou, North Bank Division, the Gambia. Our temporal address was at 5B Ingram Street in Banjul, capital of the Gambia.

Manding Medical Centre

5B Ingram Street

Banjul, The Gambia

March 2, 1993

Permanent Secretary

Ministry of Health

The Quadrangle

Banjul, The Gambia

West Africa

Dear Permanent Secretary

Re: Application for the establishment of a Medical Centre at Njawara in the North Bank.

We are pleased to bring to attention the setting up of a self-help Health organization in the North Bank Division at Njawara village. The directorates and members of the organization would be more than grateful if the Ministry of Health would allow us establish Manding Medical Centre at Njawara village, Lower Badibou District of the Gambia.

Manding Medical Centre, when fully operational, will provide medical, surgical, gynecological and obstetrics, Pediatrics and other facilities to the villagers. It will also help ease the shortage of medical facilities in that region. Manding Medical Centre will have health education secessions in the villages as an effort to enlighten our youths.

Again, thank you for taking time to consider our application and we certainly look forward to a positive recognition of the need for such a center in the rural sector of the Gambia. I am anxiously waiting to hear from your office at your convenience. Regards

Yours sincerely

Dr. Alhasan S. Ceesay, MD

Director/Coordinator

Meanwhile the villagers grew more enthused and throngs of them attended our monthly health field trips or clinics. The attendance grew so large that we ended up listing the villages to attend in turn of nine villages per trip. This usually totals to a bit above 1,000 patients at a given visit.

I normally go on weekends with three doctors and at times four volunteer doctors along with Nurses aid Mrs. Mbee Sonko and Ida Njie to assist us do the job. The field trips/clinics start with an announcement by Radio Gambia giving the names of villages expected to attend and at which village health center.

The clinic day starts with an early morning breakfast by the team and then a ride to the village health center where we would find the villagers and their sick ones assembled.

Every occasion starts with the offering of prayers and then the various village heads, in attendance help us in organizing the flow of people wanting to be seen by one of our team doctors. In most cases the day goes trouble free but at certain localities the political tension does make it very difficult to have such large groups of people without little arguments.

Thanks to the Commissioner (s) for deploying the police or making them available to quell trouble and help us maintain order during these clinics. Commissioner Lamin Koma can tell you how rough things can be at some of these clinic centers.

He was trapped in one of these bad moments of people rushing to be in the front line of the queue to see one our doctors. The Ministry of Health finally sent us the following affirmative reply as thus: -

Ministry of Health & Social services

The Quadrangle

Banjul, The Gambia

Ref.P510/289/01(95)

Dr. Alhasan Ceesay

Manding Medical Centre

5B Ingram Street

Banjul, The Gambia

RE: Application to establish a Medical Centre at Njawara

I acknowledge receipt of your letter of the 2nd March 1993 on the above-mentioned subject. I wish to inform you that this Ministry has no objection to your application to establish Manding Medical Centre at Njawara.

This initiative is in line with our national health policies and we would render our support in our joint efforts to improve the health of the people.

Signed: N. Ceesay

For Permanent Secretary.

After several more field trips it was suggested we apply for a None Governmental Organization (NGO) status. It was believed that if we become and NGO, help would come our way quicker.

I went to work on this suggestion and arranged for Tango Secretariat Centre to send one of the United Nations voluntary program officers to come and evaluate our performance relative to the objectives of Manding Medical Centre. This was accepted and a field trip was set up for September 12 to 22, 1995.

Radio Gambia made the announcement well ahead of the time for our arrival and the following was the outcome of that august gathering of September 21 &22, 1995.

Dr. Ceesay and wife Fatou Koma-Ceesay

Chapter 25

TANGO SECRETARIAT TRIP REPORT ON MANDING MEDICAL CENTRE, SEPTEMBER 21 – 22, 1995

A field trip to Kerewan at the North Bank Division was organized by the Manding Medical Centre Executive Director Dr. Alhasan S. Ceesay in conjunction with Tango Secretariat Centre to see the organization's activities and meet the members before recommending the organization as a member of Tango.

On September 21, 1995, two meetings were organized in two big centers where members gather to air their views and experience from the organization. Alkalos, chiefs, imams, women, men and youths attended these meetings. The key leadership from five villages in their speeches showed interest and support for the project and organization. Alkalo of Toro Bahen Omar Koi and chiefs donated the land for the constructing of Manding Medical Centre, the hospital and its ancillaries.

The two meeting were highly attended and successful. The Tango (UNV) program officer Mr. Muloshi on behalf of Tango gave a keynote speech on Tango's operations and activities as an umbrella organization and urged members to work hand in hand with the organization in their efforts to develop their villages and North Bank area. The three meetings with the commissioner during the field trip on our courtesy call were successful and encouraged the executive Director of Manding Medical Centre, Dr. Alhasan Ceesay, to cooperate with the strict, especially the commissioner who is one of the advisors in the local committee.

The commissioner thanked Tango for making the purpose of the mission clear to him and promised that he will try by all means to cooperate with Tango in the area of Technical advice and institution capacity building. Clinic day was organized on September 22, 1995 at Njawara and 150 people attended and got treatments.

RECOMMENDATION

Looking at the caliber of leadership and development activities compared to some NGO tango members in comparison to Manding Medical Centre, the organization need consideration since they have already activities with a promising future. Looking at the composition of the Board, they have people with a great vision. They have strong membership and backup at the grassroots levels.

The organization has chosen to do what is right at the right time and their concentration in one area is vital and a good starting point. Any success achieved by any organization depended on good leadership and discipline. Manding Medical Centre has quality leadership and deserves NGO status.

Signed: M. Muloshi

UNV Program Officer

We were delighted by the recommendation made by the United Nations voluntary Program Officer in the Gambia. We redoubled our efforts to contact organizations seeking help worldwide. In between letters and monthly field trips to different select health centers we were blessed with visits from interested friends and groups or representatives of similar organizations in the globe.

I had several telephone calls to Dr. Edward Brown, an official of the World Bank in Washington, D. C. responsible of the bank's health affairs at the time. He was very receptive and had several added discussions with Dentist Melvin George, then Director of Medical and Health Service for the Gambia, on how the bank could help in the financing of the building of Manding Medical Centre.

These talks went on well and Dr. Edward brown gave me his promise and personal commitment to helping the project and that we have to start in a small scale and the building will have to be done in several well planned phases. Dr. Sidi C. Jammeh, a former Armitage School colleague, promised to help me by constantly reminding Dr. Brown of the need to help us with the project. This kept the momentum at the World Bank alive for Manding Medical Centre.

Among our guest were a couple from Colchester, Essex, UK, Lorna V. Robinson and husband Keith Robinson were very impressed by our project and enthusiasm of the ordinary villagers about Manding Medical Centre. They fell in love with the idea and objectives of the self-help health organization and promised to help as much as they could. We had by this time submitted application for NGO status and ACCNO Secretary replied thus:

ACCNO Secretariat

Dept. of Community Development

13 Mariner Parade

Babjul, The Gambia

September 12, 1994

 Ref.CD/ACCNO/Vol3/(183)

Dr. Alhasan S. Ceesay

Director/Coordinator

Manding Medical Centre

P. O. Box 640

Banjul, The Gambia

Dear Sir,

RE: application for an NGO status within the ACCNO framework

Please find enclosed a self-explanatory letter from the Ministry for local government and lands concerning the approval of your application for NGO status.

ACCCNO Secretariat congratulates your organization for successfully completing the registration process and wishes you a fruitful relationship in the field of development.

Thank you for your cooperation

Yours Faithfully

Musu Ngujo

For: ACCNO desk Officer

Cc: file & R/File

Replies from our worldwide appeal letters did not pour in money nor did they materialized beyond promises to help in due course. Hence, I decided to open up a pharmacy at my expense at my residence in the Bundung area of Serekunda using the proceeds from its sales to finance the health field trips and activities of the organization.

This meant spending an extra three to fours at the pharmacy daily after eight hours at the RVH before rejoining my family. All drugs used for the treatment of patients at our field trip clinics were purchased from sales I made at the Bundung Pharmacy.

A local agency, known as IBAS, lent me D8000, interest free, which was used in buying drugs and paying for transportation for the project's activities.

The loan was completely repaid well ahead of the allowed sixteen months period given by IBAS. We are obliged and grateful to Aja Ndey Oley Jobe and management of IBAS for their kindness to assist us at the time.

Just when things were about to be financially complete for us to start the first phase of building the various sections of the hospital, came the unexpected coup d'etat of July 22, 1994. The reaction from would be our donors and supporters or sponsors were swift and equally unexpected.

All those who were considering giving the project a chance sited likelihood of sudden national unrest and instability as reasons for their withdrawal of promised aid and participation while some suggested my waiting until after the transition phase of the coup d'etat before they would reconsider reopening our files with them.

Again it resorted to legend or case of the chicken the egg, which came first as no one, knew when the transition would end and we kept our fingers crossed hoping that daylight will be ours in not far distance.

It was a severe blow to our hope and for getting the type of interest and support that was engendered for Manding Medical Centre would be difficult to match after such crisis that occurred in the Gambia. Many were acting in conjunction with their governments, which were not sure of what the future under military rule would be for the Gambia.

All prospective and possible international sources earmarked for Manding Medical Centre were either frozen or evaporated into thin air with the coup leaving me floating in the middle of the ocean of despair without a life jacket except God's merciful hands. I knew the villagers would grow restless if nothing happens in the direction of building the center.

I called an emergency general meeting with members from most of the villages and told them of the new challenge and development and this information not only fell on deaf ears but left their spirits dampened. Interest waxed and waned at some quarters but I kept on trying my best not to be despondent like the others have shown.

I kept the organization alive under very limited funds raised from the pharmacy at Bundung until my trip to the UK in January 2000. Before leaving the Gambia, the Commissioner for north Bank Division and chairman of the local advisory committee for Manding Medical Centre, Mr. Lamin Koma, gave me the following letter to assist me in my fund raising drive while in England and possible other European countries. It read thus:

The Commissioner

Kerewan Village

North Bank Division

The Gambia, West Africa

June 15, 1998

TO WHOM IT MAY CONCERN

I hereby write to testify and confirm that Manding Medical Centre is a self-help health project situated at Njawara village, North Bank Division.

As the Commissioner of this division I was elected as the Chairman of the local advisory Committee of the Manding Medical Centre. As I am concerned, I am aware of this self-help project since it took off the ground, by the able hands of Dr. Alhasan S. Ceesay, a born citizen of Njawara village.

The purpose of the establishing of such a medical centre is to provide medical attention/care to all Gambians irrespective of religion, tribe, nationality or gender and age within the country and sub-region.

It is in these regards that this office writes to seek for your assistance in providing support in cash/kind to make this medical center a reality. I look forward to your continued support and cooperation.

Signed: V. Baldeh

For Commissioner

North Bank Division

Mrs. Binta Ceesay, Sister

The new millennium started with good omen for Manding Medical Centre. I have been invited to go to Europe and America on a found raising trip for the center but could not because of my commitment with the Royal Victoria Hospital (RVH). I needed a longer vacation period to be able to travel and keep my job at the sane time.

Above all my family needed the monetary support, which would fade away if I lost the post at the RVH. Hence, to my delight and greatest timely occurrence I heard from my long-standing friend in Colchester, Mrs. Lorna V. Robinson, inviting my wife and I to come to the UK to attend the wedding of their younger daughter on January 9th, 2000.

Coincidentally, I had just started my annual leave, which was to finish on the 26th of January 2000. The excitement mounted when we received a fax from the visa officer at the British High Commission in the Gambia requesting that we report to the visa processing office with our passports on Tuesday 8.30 am January 4th, 2000 for processing of our visas for our pending travels to the UK.

This took me by surprise because of the casual way we had discussed the possibility of such a trip. So when we got the telephone call followed by the said fax from the visa section I was caught off guard and had to rush through all the preparations for my wife and I to travel to UK without a second thought on whether adequate arrangements were being made for my eventual pursuit of a postgraduate degree (MRCP) in internal medicine.

Hind side has it that I needed to discuss this aspect with the visa councilor and request for eventual student visa status or leave to remain until my completion of the post graduate degree I wanted to pursue.

Miss Famatanding Ceesay, Daughter

God's ways and timing are best for every occasion. I was yearning to get a way out of the financial limbo the center ran into since the change of government in the Gambia. Now that opportunity was suddenly thrown on my laps by Lorna Robinson's open-ended invitation for my wife and to attend their daughter's wedding ceremony in the UK.

Interested donors started being weary about Military rule and possible restlessness that may ensue. Hence, Manding Medical Centre literally lost all its prospective overseas support as well as sponsors most of who had cold feet after the July coup detaches of 2004.

I ended up running the center from my meager salary of D1500 or seventy-five pounds sterling per month and of literally hard labor with long hours at a time. The other source was from what little I could make from sales at the Bundung pharmacy.

To cut a long story short we were granted visas to travel to the UK. We left the Gambia on the 6th of January 2000 on a new footing and challenge to bring back some life into Manding Medical center while in England.

I got on the ball as soon as the wedding ceremony was over. I obtained a three–year study leave from the Management Board of the Royal Victoria Hospital in Banjul.

This gave me all the time I needed to try to rekindle interest in the center and thereby inject into Manding Medical center cash flow it needed to help us meet or our targeted goal and objective for the farming community in the North Bank Division of the Gambia.

It was more like a miracle entering this new concrete and direct ways. Help from my host Lorna Robinson of Colchester, Essex, UK further anointed my hands. Lorna and I wrote several letters to various places, including celebrities and organizations, most of who replied in the negative because of perception they had about the political climate in Gambia since the coup d'etat of July 22nd 1994.

Nonetheless some hinted being interested at a later date, meaning when the solders return to camp. A few donated small amounts plus hospital items. By now it became clear that we have to counter the perception most, on this side of the isles feel or had about the Gambia at the time.

This dreadful start did not alarm me much for I am fully aware of the wrong information about the average African in the village, who like most, is just a decent human being trying to earn an honest living for himself, family and community. Villagers are least interested in all the political gimmickry shrouding and clothing their lives.

I do not at all blame the rest of world for getting sick and tired of helping and not seeing any tangible good come out of it and worse some African politicians and regimes show no interest in helping move the African people onto better and modern rewarding modalities of life.

They offer more lip service than opening avenues for progress. How many knew that the Ethiopian starvation was politically orchestrated by the then Mangestu regime? Genocide regime and the heartlessness of some African politicians made me feel sick.

To remove any possible skeptics regarding Manding Medical Centre and its objectives we decided to have it registered as a charitable organization in the UK under the name of Colchester Friends of Manding charitable trust. The Robinson knew a solicitor who would be so kind to help us with the legal aspect of the registration process with UK charity Commission.

They spoke to Mr. Bruce Ballard of the Birkett long Solicitors to come to our aid. This kind gentleman, like my lawyer friend, Mr. Ousainou Darboe, gladly agreed to help and sent us a draft of the Trust deed.

After a series of changes were made on the draft he forwarded our request to be registered in the UK as a charitable organization helping its twin partner or parent group, Manding Medical Centre at Njawara village in the Gambia, West Africa.

Meanwhile, we concentrated our activities through media campaign effort to call attention to existence of Friends of Manding and their desire in building a hospital for Manding Medical Centre at Njawara, the Gambia. Again we ran into a very gentle heart in the person of Miss Helen Anderson of Colchester who was the Community website editor for Essex County.

She went head over heels regarding the idea of helping others so far away when approached by Lorna Robinson. Helen thought the idea wonderful and at the same time helped us have our own website and also had an article published by the Evening Gazette which had a large reader circulation.

In the same vein I got the interest of Dr. Linda Mahon-Daly, Dr. Peter Wilson, Dr. Laurel Spooner, Dr. Richard Spooner, Dr. Philip Murray, Dr. Barbara Murray, Dr. Fredric Payne, who by the way was our Medical superintendent under who I worked at the RVH during the later part of colonial Gambia, along with many surgeries in the Colchester area.

These were my Good Samaritans of the day who worked acidulously to make Manding Medical Centre become a reality for the villagers in the Gambia. Dr. Linda Mahon-Daly helped distribute letters about Manding Medical Centre to nearly all her colleagues in the Colchester Borough and so did Dr. Laurel Spooner. Bless their hearts for kindness and job well done. The news article published by the Evening Gazette brought us another very helpful and kind person, Mr. Malkait singh who is an ophthalmologist and had made several trips to the Gambia before knowing about the Friends of Manding. He was delighted to join Neville Thompson, Connie Thompson, Lorna Robinson, Keith Robinson, Leonard Thompson, Mark Naylor, Barbara Philips and others as pioneering members of Friends of Manding. Mr. Malkait Singh and I grew to be very good friends and he had since given me lots of personal monetary help to cater for my exams and family back in the Gambia.

I am very grateful for interest and kindness, and concern he showed about my family. A few months after the formation of Friends of Manding, Dr. Laurel Spooner spent a week in the Gambia vacationing and doing some fact finding about the center. During which time she visited Manding Medical Centre at Njawara in the North Bank Division.

The villagers were happy to meet her and thanked her about good work being done in Colchester regarding Manding Medical Centre. Everyone was happy about the news that people in the UK were poised to assist Manding Medical Centre goes forward in its drive to provide medical aid to villagers.

A meeting of member of the Friends of Manding was scheduled for the first week of February 2001. Mean while our solicitor continued pressing for registration of Friends of Manding, which is the arm and Manding Medical Centre's Colchester branch support group, as charity in the UK.

Dr. Laurel Spooner suggested we start with small-scale form of the center and then gradually expand as funds become available. This consideration would be studied in full and deliberated upon by the committee during the forth-coming February meeting.

Miss Binta Ceesay, Daughter

Chapter 26

WHAT IS MANDING MEDICAL CENTRE?

Manding Medical Centre, located at Njawara village in the North Bank Region, Gambia, West Africa, is a self-help village health organization founded by Dr. Alhasan S. Ceesay. Its objective is to provide medical service to the villagers by providing efficient and affordable medical aid to all people in and around the Gambia, especially the rural sector.

We are dedicated to relieving suffering and ensure effective treatment for villagers and all attending Manding Medical Centre at Njawara, NBR.

ESTABLISHED

The Manding Medical Centre is founded by Dr. Alhasan Sisawo Ceesay, a native of Njawara village in 1992, because of sheer shortage of medical service to the region and the preponderance of premature deaths by children from Malaria, malnutrition, diarrhea, and worm infestations.

These childhood maladies account for almost 25% of Gambian children's death before the ripeful age of five years. The Gambia Ministry of Health officially recognized the Centre in 1995 and prior to which it became a none Governmental Organization (NGO) on September 12th, 1994.

In addition, the Manding Medical Centre now has Friends of Manding Charitable Trust, Colchester, Essex, UK as its arm and liaison in the UK and the European Union countries. The Friends of Manding is a registered charity in England and Wales. Its registration number is 1088136 since August 21, 2001.

In similar development and purpose, Dr. Avery Aten heads the Friends of Manding Alpena Charitable Trust, Alpena, Michigan, UAS since May 2005.

MISSION STATEMENT

Suffering in another human being is a call to the rest of us to stand in fellowship. It requires us to be there and it is a mystery, which demands the spirit of caring, sharing and our presence. Our duty as healthcare professionals is providing medical care, which is a fundamental right of all human beings.

This village health organization is dedicated to providing medical aid to the rural sector and farming community in the Gambia. It will compliment the health service in the Gambia in addition it will promote preventive medicine in the hinterland of the Gambia.

MEMBERSHIP

Well over twenty thousand villagers, comprising of farmers, village heads, and chiefs, the Kerewan Area Council, Commissioners and local District Authority are now fully active enthusiastic members of Manding Medical Centre. All are welcomed to join the endeavors of the center. People from the rest of the globe are more than welcomed to participate or share with us our dream in bring much needed medical service to people in desperate state because of lack of medical facilities.

ACTIVITIES

Manding Medical Centre tries to alleviate some of the above mentioned health problems and situations by having bimonthly health field trips/clinics to villages teaching them about health, preventive medicine and hygiene that would help reduce the number infected and the vectors responsible for these diseases.

We encourage antenatal and postnatal attendance of clinics by mothers and we treat the sick amongst them with minimum charge to not so elderly and pregnant young ladies. The service is free to children, the very elderly, and the indigent needing emergency treatment. The rest pay amounts well below tat in private practice. Money accrued is subsequently used to buy drugs with which to treat the patients and for other projects of the center.

When in cession the center treats well more than 1000 patients per field trip to the villages. We provide free information and advisory service on aids and sexually transmitted diseases (STDs) to the young, all patients, their relatives and friends. We also plan to have a Nursing School in due course to augment not only staff but also the government health centers when the need arises.

Bintou Ceesay bu Ismaila Ceesay and her husband 2016

Chapter 27

IMMEDIATE GOAL AND APPEAL

The villagers are very enthused about the center and Toro Bahen village, next to Njawara village, has donated two plots of land for the building of the center and its ancillary units, which is now leased to manding medical center for ninety-nine years.

More than 2000 children die tragically from malaria and other childhood ailments stated above for shortage of health services. We are eager to start building the children' and maternity wings of the proposed Gambia General Hospital at Manding Medical Centre and do need raise the required 900,000 pounds sterling to accomplish our goal.

Ten bags of cement cost thirty pounds sterling or $60 (sixty us dollars). Also we would be most grateful if we could be assisted with medicines and equipment to facilitate our work. Hence we implore you to kindly support our yearning to build the children' and maternity wings of Manding Medical Centre. We are dedicated to providing medical aid to the villager, especially children.

We are investors in people and you are invited to join the endeavors of Manding Medical Centre at Njawara village, the Gambia, West Africa.

Help us make a difference and beacon of hope for the villagers. Please give generously. Today's hope can be tomorrow's reality. We want to contribute positively towards the health services of the Gambia, and with this center in place it will create greater health awareness and privation by the villagers.

Cash contributions of any amount should be sent in the name of Manding Medical Centre, to the Friends of Manding charitable Trust, 82 Finchingfield Way, Blackheath, Colchester, Essex, CO2 OAU, and England. It is vital to be certain that Dr. Alhasan S. Ceesay is informed of your contribution via email thus: alhasanceesay@hotmail.com

Your kindness and humane consideration to help save lives will always be deeply appreciated and grateful for by the villagers, the Gambia and I.

Mrs. Fatou Koma Ceesay, Oldham, UK 2017

Chapter 28

OVERSEASES LINKS

The Friends of Manding in Colchester, Essex County, UK, is formed by a local group of residents, doctors, and nurses who regularly visited the Gambia and is in support of Manding Medical Centre. Manding medical center through the auspices of the Friends of Manding recently received recognition and registration by the UK Charity Commission.

They serve as support and our liaison in the Europe Union. The Friends of Manding in behalf of Manding Medical Centre at Njawara has been entered in the central Register of charities with effect from August 21, 2001; the registration number is 1088136 for England and Wales.

Also, a similar charitable trust, the Alpena Friends of Manding Charitable Trust of Michigan, USA, has been established in Alpena, Michigan in June 2006. It's headed by Dr. Avery Aten a resident physician chairman of the Women and newborn of the Alpena region Community Health along with the medical community of Alpena.

Chapter 29

MANDING MEDICAL CENTRE MILESTONES

Manding Medical Centre has been in my mind's drawing board since the early 1950s but it took off in earnest when I returned to the Gambia, after graduating from medical school in 1992. The Centre is registered as a charity with the Attorney general's Office, Department of Justice, Banjul, The Gambia, since 1993. The Gambia Ministry of Health also recognized it in the same year.

Toro Bahen village, Lower Badibou, NBD, Gambia, donated two huge plots of land for the location of the center in 1993. Our none governmental (NGO) status was approved in 1994. On September 21, 1995 Tango Secretariat sent a United Nations voluntary program Officer, Mr. Muloshi on field trip to evaluate the organizational and extent of support for Manding Medical Centre at Njawara village.

Mr. Muloshi's recommendation after two days field trip to the region stated thus; "Looking at the caliber of leadership and development activities to some NGO Tango members in comparison to Manding Medical Centre, the organization need consideration since they have already activities with a promising future. Looking at composition of the Board, they have people with a vision.

They have strong membership and backup at grass root levels. The organization has chosen to what is right at the right time and their concentration in one area is vital and good starting point. Any success achieved by any group or organization depends on good leadership and discipline.

Manding Medical Centre has high quality leadership and deserves NGO status". It was not until my travels to the UK in 2000 that the Friends of Manding Charitable Trust was formed and registered as charity in England and Wales by the UK Charity Commission.

Friends of Manding is the extended arm of Manding Medical Centre at Njawara, The Gambia. They serve as our liaison in the UK and the European Union. Please browse on our website thus: http://friendsofmandinggambimed.btck.co.uk, to learn more or for further information about our work and organization. We are still on fund raising activities to earn enough to enable us build the children' and maternity units of the hospital at Manding Medical Centre at Njawara.

In May 2005, 11 American students and their instructor Mr. Thomas Ray visited Manding Medical Centre at Njawara. Additionally, input from has now resulted in Alpena City, Michigan, USA, twining by proclamation with Njawara and Kinte kunda villages in Gambia respectively on the 5th of December 2005. In June 2006, Dr. Avery Aten, Chairman of the Women and Newborn of Alpena Region Health Community along with the medical community of Alpena commenced processing application for a charitable Trust to be named Alpena friends of Manding Charitable Trust, Michigan, USA.

This will soon be finalized and up and running to help Dr. Alhasan Ceesay in the provision of medicine and educational assistance to schools in the Lower Badibou district, the Gambia, West Africa.

In August 2008, Dr. Alhasan Ceesay and the Badibou Cultural Dance Troupe will visit Alpena and other cities in Michigan for fund raising drive to enable the building of the Manding Medical Centre children and maternity units at Njawara village.

Dr. Richard Bates, an Obynge, and a number of medical professionals involved in obstetrics and gynecology at Alpena, Michigan joined Manding Medical Centre's crusade on 17/08/07.

Chapter 30

TEMPLATE FOR REGIONAL DEVELOPMENT

Manding Medical Centre became a template for districts elsewhere and villagers to nurture, develop further and handover to the next generation. This None Governmental Health Organization epitomizes a developmental watchtower for the region.

Manding medical center (at Njawara village) is now a pulsating source of hope for jobs, training and superb medical service to the region. Everyone knows that government alone does not move things fast enough. Society must be radical and pragmatic to pitch into its development.

We know all too well that the developed world got where its because private efforts were self prophetic and projects like Manding Medical Centre goes long ways to initiate and stimulate community to work together for a positive agenda for its people.

Hence after many years of foot dragging and vicissitude by society I decided I will build the hospital if I have to single-handed. I worked years receiving no government assistance and without grants from the great of the Gambian community. Manding Medical Centre is a positive good that help our regions to cross the road to a better healthcare delivery.

We thank everyone for making it possible that our center became a platform and guide in rejuvenating our regions. We now provide medical service to all Gambians and none Gambians domiciled in the Gambia. We will create more jobs as need arises.

This was the reason why I gave my life's comfort for reward that will benefit most needy villagers. It came through determination and kindness of many people worldwide. There are some things only governments can do but together communities through collective initiatives can achieve at least fifty percent of their developmental needs in addition to government effort.

Today some see Manding medical centre as perpetual monument of good, an honor to the country and a general benefit to villagers and children in the North Bank of the Gambia. Manding medical centre is an inspiration and cause for thankfulness and celebration.

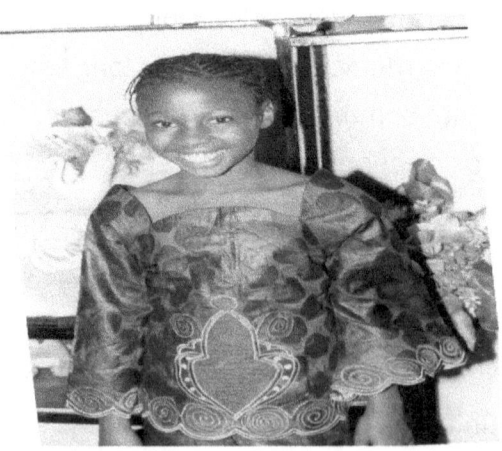

Miss Roheyata Ceesay, Daughter

Chapter 31
AN APPEAL TO INTERNATIONAL COMMUNITY

Dear Readers,

The above information about Manding Medical Centre is included in this work only hoping that it will help spread the word more extensively and draw awareness to a greater community of people and readers of my work. It's my belief that lots of good people out there may want to participate or give to the cause and goal of the center should they be aware of its existents for the villagers.

Hence, I am appealing for help and participatory support from all able to extend their hearts to make this much needed medical endeavor to come to fruition for the rural sector of the Gambia.

Who knows you might even end up coming to bask in our beautiful seaside and relish Gambian generosity. Music for me is reaching out to help others and my patients are yearning for your kind participation and donation in cash/kind.

Thanks a million for considering our appeal. God blesses your heart(s). I write with believe that by it money can be generated to provide a much needed medical service to the rural sector. Writing about the Manding Medical Centre may course some Good Samaritan and any wanting to leave foot prints on the sand of time for a good cause to come to our assistance to help us meet the goals of the center at Njawara village, the Gambia, West Africa. My head, heart and soul are devoted to my family, the Gambia and Manding Medical Centre.

It is not a God given calling but a mere conviction that our rural folks deserve better health service than currently available and hence human calling to want to contribute positively to bring resolution of some of our rural health service inadequacies.

I never had an angel come down to me nor have I ever heard the voices of God saying, "Ceesay, you must do so and so" as many mocked Manding Medical Centre emanated from sheer conviction that it is a dutiful way of doing the right thing for curbing premature deaths of children before reaching 5 years of life from malaria, water born diseases, and warm infestations; and in the same vein providing both pre and postnatal care to the pregnant.

Hence, portions of proceeds of sales in all my work go to help meet the center's operational costs and in providing scholarship to indigent indigenous rural candidates due course return to serve rural Gambia wishing to read for a medical degree or agriculture and Medicine.

Signed: Dr. Alhasan S. Ceesay, MD

Email: alhasanceesay@hotmail.com

Chapter 32

LORNA ROBINSON, AN ANGEL OF MERCY

Keith, Dr. Ceesay, and late Lorna Robinson

There are certain moulds God broke them moments after He finished making them. Mrs. Lorna V. Robinson was one of these unique, caring, sharing and rare angels of mercy.

Mrs. Lorna Robinson and I met through her job as general nurse at the then Essex County General hospital in Colchester, Essex County in 1990, when I was a trainee doctor at the hospital. She and husband Keith Robinson became my friends as far back as in the 1990s and one of their annual pilgrimages is visiting my family in the Gambia, West Africa.

This benevolent couple has since been my Colchester if not my England. Together we set to catch a dream of providing medical aid and service to Gambian villagers. I left at the end of my training to serve my country in 1992. In December 1999 Mrs. Lorna Robinson sent an invitation for my wife and I to attend wedding of Miss Fiona Robinson, her younger daughter, to gentleman Reeves.

We have since 2000 worked acidulously to make the above goal come to fruition, especially for those in the rural sector of the North Bank Region of the Gambia. It was Lorna's joint effort with, nurses, Doctors Laurel Spooner, Barbara Murray, Richard Spooner, Phil Murray, Linda Mahon-Daly, Peter R. Wilson, Malkait Singh and residents of Colchester, which lead to the formation of the Colchester Friends of Manding Charitable Trust.

It was registered as a charity in England and Wales in 2001. The charity number is 1088136.This charity acts as liaison in the European Union countries for Manding Medical Centre at Njawara village in the Badibous of the North Bank Region, the Gambia.

Since its conception, the Friends of Manding Charitable Trust had busied itself on weekly or bimonthly Gambi-barzaars in an effort to help raise money for building of both the children and maternity units of the center.

Mrs. Lorna Robinson spent countless week-ends either selling material such as toys, coats and anything she could lay her hands on as long as she believes it will generate money for the building of the children and maternity units of the center.

She spent most of her retirement time organizing activity for the center to help promote our cause. She sent books, spectacles, pens and pencils along with medication for the center's use.

The influence of this Good Samaritan group in Colchester reverberated and lead to the formation of a similar charity group in America, which is lead by Dr. Avery Aten, Alpena Friends of Manding Charitable Trust, Michigan, USA, was formed in May 2005.

All this came about because Mrs. Lorna V. Robinson, the lady of mercy bchind the wheel, would not rest while the indigent goes without the most basic things in life. Here is how Lorna views her part during one of many conversations we had about the need to share worth and ourselves with other less fortunate than us.

She simply said, "Ceesay, I feel delighted and warm at heart in helping others, like the villagers. I strongly belief good used could be made from my work and experience I had at the NHS over years. I will try to recruit as many retired nurses to our cadre as long as they listen to my please.

The other secrete is that such activity keeps me young, participating and contributing to the needy. I feel alive and forever growing. In life we most extend our hearts to others and with compassion reach the needy."

This tit bit tells about the unselfish nature of Mrs. Lorna V. Robinson who through the years since her retirement gave her all to help others, especially the villagers, breath a sigh of relief and to have hope and knowledge that someone far away they never met cared about them.

Lorna continued saying, "It brings joy to my heart when I share the little I have with the needy. It helps to uplift the despondent. Millions suffer needlessly for not having means of proper health care, clean and safe water, good shelter and chance to attend schools.

I want to help you get the villagers from a downward spiral of deepening health deprivation. I certainly take hope in people like you and your stand to help your folks back home in the Gambia." It was this unique caring angel that I lost on the third of March 2010 for she returned peacefully to her maker on this day. The above was my Lorna and now I cry, when shall we be blessed will another like her?

Losing Lorna Robinson left me feeling that I lost the best person, outside of my family, I ever known. She was a kind soul of unswerving determination to share the little She had with the little guy needing her help.

She stood by my cause in thick and thin moments of my stay in the United Kingdom.

Dr. Alhasan S. Ceesay graduating from the American University of the Caribbean, West Indies, 1992

The provision of medical care to villagers is more than a responsibility; it is a sacred trust for me. I will not the villagers or memory Mrs. Lorna V. Robinson down because I believe in looking to the well being of the less fortunate. One carries on trying on reflecting on all the children and villagers who need this health care. Hence no trepidation will hold me back.

My family, the villagers and I miss and deeply mourn her premature departure from mother earth. May she rest in peace with her maker and may we the living without fail or fear able to follow the high shining examples of indefatigable Good Samaritan she was in life.

I hope you will join me to keep her memory and legacy alive for other to copy while we continue taking medical aid to villagers in rural Gambia. Lorna V. Robinson thanks a million and goodbye for now.

Signed: Dr. Alhasan S. Ceesay, MD

Manding Medical Centre, Njawara

The Gambia, West Africa. E-mail: alhasanceesay@hotmail.com

Dr. Blais Tambo and family, Manchester UK, 2017

Chapter 33

MY SAMARITAN MEN OF GOOD WILL

Every successful person had Samaritan angels who offered their shoulders for him or her to stand on and see further than most. Compiled herein are my Samaritan men of goodwill. Hence, I beg leave to indulge in a bit of sentimentality about a few rare human angels who played major part in today's success and help for my villagers.

Believe me their moulds, as you will soon find, are beyond those of simple people. These men help me reach today's pedestal. In medicine for the villager, I profiled ladies who championed my cause. Now, bear with me for just a few lines on the Samaritan men of goodwill.

They like the previously mentioned ladies al not only believe in my dream and objective for the villager but also gave all they could to help make that dream come to fruition. These men gave unparalleled needed help and friendship to me when I was distressed and in utter despair and darkness.

Some even shed a few tears with me because the pain and set back certain roadblocks caused my goal. One of these was the day I received GMC' e-mail of the 17th June 2008 recanting recognition of my primary medical qualification based on frivolous website enter.

Hell brewed to its hottest temperatures, as it took time to unravel the misunderstanding, before GMC rectified the error. However, with your indulgence let us start from the beginning of the geneses.

It was with God' anointing hand in conjunction with Sisawo Bajo Ceesay, alias Sisawo Salah) that my twin partner I landed on this Garden of Eden. Father gave us love and good guidance throughout his life with us. He and I had deferent perception about western Education and culture but we reconciled after my completing primary school at Kinte Kunda.

My father's experience from the hands of colonials made him never to entertain idea of his progeny deviating from the farmers' mold. Nor would he allow me pursue Western Education and ideology, which at the time was alien to my father and his peers.

He once told me: Son, my wish for you is to be a hard working good farmer and not indulge in the quagmire and sleaze world of spin-doctors. I do not want you tinkering with ideology that would infuse into you wrong philosophies about life and God.

My father came from a different generation with totally different perceptions about invaders ruling them. Let us for a moment step into their shoes to find out why the resistance for their progeny to attend school. In my father's days men believed in God, the sanctity of life and peaceful coexistence of the communities they lived. About the invading longhaired men he calls devils, father said: "Son the way these men, meaning the colonialist, took over our countries can only be the work of the devil. They came from the blue sea and seized our land and minerals, and remaining on the best parts while leaving us the worst places to farm and for our animals to grace.

To pour oil on fire they requested that we change our religions and ways to their dark and indiscipline life styles. To top up, our people were forced to live under laws promulgated by the invaders on top of which we must pay to learn their languages while they make systemic concerted efforts to distorted and destroy everything that was dear to us.

They massacred, disgraced, and dethroned all our kings and chiefs. These shameful acts were reinforced with policies of divide and rule by pitting tribe against tribe and even bribing those bad elements willing to do their dirty work. Wages paid to workers were not worth the coin they were minted on.

They made certain no organization, political or professional civil service existed in our countries". He said, "They filled the jails with those of us who refused to be indoctrinated or accept the supremacy of the foreign invaders.

So Son, because of kindheartedness and gentled nature of the African our ways are undermined and thrown out by invaders who replaced it with greed, unkindness, spin-doctoring, and lack of respect for man and nature.

He concluded by saying, these are just a few reasons why I would not let my blood attend school". The above is a pinhole view of father's radicalism and patriotic views. He did recap late later in his old age and finally gave full blessings to my efforts and future goals.

He passed away peacefully to his maker in 1991 while I was a trainee doctor doing my clinical clerkship rotation at Colchester General Hospital in Colchester, Essex County, England. Notices no matter how simple were just bundles of scribbles on worthless paper to the farmer. The illiterates who cannot decipher the prints are cheated of their rights and land.

I was not going to be among those who cannot decipher the print and hence found my way to Kinte Kunda Primary School where I met with the head Master, Mr. Louis Albert Bouvier, who hails from Banjul, our capital city. This benevolent teacher was my first real contact with Western Education and we gelled instantly and became inseparable.

He allowed me to stay at his home and treated me as his own son. He was kind and firm and wasted no time teaching me about life and on how to compete without strangulating the competitor. He told me repeatedly that competition was a healthy fund and stressed that one must be honest and have integrity and tolerance in life. He counseled hard work at everything one did. Above all, it was incumbent on me to have faith and to serve God daily, if not more but never less.

Also he allowed me all the freedom a growing child needed without pampering me. He did lay certain straightforward and simple rules for me. I was to study at a designated time, return home in time whenever I went into town, unless given an extension by him, and to be in bed by 10:00 pm, with lights off whether sleepy or not. He insisted that I perform my five daily prayers as expected of my religion even though he was devoured Catholic.

Mr. Bouvier would only help with my homework when he felt that I have done my best at it and that I was not trying to have him do the work. Otherwise, he would let me go and make a fool of myself before the class before I deserve his coveted help.

Hash you think but this strict beginning or treatment, as you would call it, made me do well at school and do things with confidence independently at very tender age. I remain profoundly grateful to Mr. Louis Albert Bouvier for being educational springboard, for being a sincere and true friend and mentor.

Something said by Francis Farmer summed up the relationship between L. A. Bouvier and me. She said, "To have a good friend is the purest of all God' gifts, for it is a love that has no exchange of payments.

It is not inherited, as with family. It is not compelling, as with a child. And it has no means of physical pleasures, as with a mate. It is, therefore, an indescribable bond that brings with it a far deeper devotion than others".

Mr. L. A Bouvier continued to help and mold my academic life until when I started Armitage School in 1957. Leaving a friend like Mr. Bouvier was difficult and emotional for both of us. We have become one and are now to say farewell and perhaps separate forever.

He prepared me well but like any parent or true friend he worried about the difficulties that lay ahead. I just wished they had transferred him with me to Armitage. On the day I boarded the land rover to Armitage tears rundown Mr. Bouvier's cheeks and mother turned her head away to hide her own.

L. A. Bouvier was my best friend, after the loss of my twin brother, fate had it that I was now about to be far away from all I knew and loved. Mr. L. A. Bouvier kept cautioning me to, "keep your head up and do your school works. You have never been a failure, and even if such a sad experience occurs, keep trying over and over to overcome it.

We send you to Armitage with prayers, pride and above all with our deepest love. May God keep you in good health. Goodbye, Mr. Ceesay." It was very moving for this was the first time he addressed me as Mr. Ceesay. We boarded the Land Rover and as it started to move Bouvier followed for some distance exhorting me not to fear to ask for help when need arose.

He kept saying he would gladly help or would ask my parents to pitch in whenever possible. Mr. L. A. Bouvier and I kept in touch despite the distance poor mail service of those days. The link continued while I was in the USA. I lost my friend in a motorcar accident, six year before returning from America in 1974.

His vehicle is said to have ran off the road went over a hill. Another part of me went with him. The evil that men do lives after them and the good is interred with their bodies. Well rest assured that L. A. Bouvier's good deeds did remain alive and intact on earth.

At Armitage it was a newly qualified teaches from Kaur, Mr. Keko B. A. Manneh, who then doubled as our class' English and Mathematic teacher that filled in gap left by my leaving L. A. Bouvier at Kinte Kunda. He was soft-spoken Chaucerian, a nickname we gave him because he crammed the entire work of Chaucer. He too loved me and was a good guide at Arbitrage.

I am grateful for encouragement and help he gave and for really being there when I needed an honest person to open up to about difficulty or academic aspiration. I left for New York on the 24 August 1967 and arrived at Alpena Michigan 1:30 Am on the 25 August 1967.

Mr. Henry V. Vali, a counselor and foreign student advisor at Alpena Community College, was at the bus station to pick me. After the formality of welcoming to Alpena he drove me to 251 Washington Avenue the home of Mr. Howard Riggs where it had been agreed I stay until start of the semester in September before moving to Russell Wilson Hall at the Alpena Community College campus.

Not surprising Mr. Vali and I became friends and remained so ever since. Mr. Howard Riggs and family welcomed me home as late as it was on that glorious day when I set foot in Michigan.

They were all delighted to have me in their lovely home and they gave me princely meal to nourish my body and milk to quench my thirst. Howard owned Ice-Cream Pallor down Town. He was very modest, delightful man and above all a very generous person.

Soon Mr. and Mrs. Riggs became mom and dad throughout my American stay for their overwhelmingly kind people deserving such salutation from a poor villager.

Howard's warmth and generosity to other made his family unique company to foreign students coming to Alpena. The Riggs were the ideal Americans to me. They were average working family who readily shared the little bit God gave them with others less fortunate. I remained grateful to these kind-hearted friends.

Mr. Vali and Mr. Thomas Rither, Director of Foreign students at Alpena Community College, and I met several time to discuss my financial nightmare. Mr. Rither was too concerned that the college might face INS censor if he allowed my staying without a sponsor or means to pay fees and cater for myself.

He was adamant and made it very clear to me that failure to get help for the first semester will leave him with no other option but to advise the immigration to consider deporting proceedings against me.

He gave a week ultimatum for me to sort things out before our next meeting 18 September 1967. Copies of letters from my would be sponsor, Mr. Isdor Gold, never move or evoke sympathy from him as he epidermises a true inelastic bureaucrat.

Mr. Henry V. Vali convinced Mr. Thomas Rither to hold on while get in touch with some residents about my case. He was on the telephone to different would be possible sympathizers to my cause.

Most of who agreed to contribute toward the cost of my first semester at Alpena Community College. Vali also spoke to the president of the college in my behalf to prevent Mr. Rither from hastily and unilaterally contacting the INS for frivolous fears in his head.

My plight soon became a house whole affair and many residents pitched in to help resolve the case. Mr. Vali, Mrs. Glennie spearheaded the appeal and very soon it snowballed letting me start my first semester at Alpena Community College, in Alpena, Michigan.

Fr. John miller at St. Bernard Rectory in Alpena not only lent me $250 but evangelized my state in every sermon for three weeks netting me much needed financial help. God bless his heart. He left Alpena before my transfer to Olivet College in Olivet Michigan in 1979.

Judge Philip Glennie was head of the 26th circuit Court of Michigan at the time. His wife, Mrs. Viola Gennie, was professor of foreign language at Alpena Community College. Both not only contributed substantial amounts towards my tuition but also became my adopted parents in Alpena.

They continued to link with me like wise support my goal until their return to heaven in the late nineties. I remember these friends with joy mingled with sadness that they are not here to share reward they showed but also I remember them with intense gratitude for role and kindness shown me while a student at Alpena Community College, Alpena, Michigan, USA. In another vein Alpena Community College gave me part time job at the Library and a summer job at the Salmon Experimental Fish hatchery. Thanks to grand efforts of Mr. Henry V. Vali and residents of Alpena I was able to overcome the financial crisis of my first semester at the college.

L – R: Dr. Alhasan S. Ceesay, Prof. Sul S. Nyang, Mr. Cloyd Ramsey and Prof. Francis Conti, 1984

I met Mr. Cloyd Ramsey while seeking a summer job at the Medical Arts Clinic in Alpena. He was then manager of the unit at the time. Upon hearing my plight he promised to see what he could do even though the clinic itself had no jobs openings for that summer.

I left him impressed and very moved by what he heard. He too became an integral part of my time and sojourner in America than any through contributions and loans he took from the Alpena bank in my behalf to support my studies throughout my stay in the USA and short stay in Liberia, West Africa.

It was through kindness of Mr. Ramsey and his sponsorship that enabled Michigan Technological University at Houghton to accept me do a Masters program in Biological Sciences from 1971 to 1973. It was Mr. Cloyd Ramsey who came to my rescuer when things went very bad and unbearable and practically unsafe for me after the military coup d'etat against William Tolbert' administration of Liberia in 1981.

He provided a round trip Air ticket to the USA and supporting it with invitation for me as their guest at Sandusky, Michigan December 1981. The invitation secured me a B-2 Visa to Detroit, Michigan. I arrived in New York 1:15 pm 20 December 1981.

I prayed on disembarking and I was grateful and thankful to God and Cloyd Ramsey having set foot once more on US soil. I thanked Cloyd Ramseyceaselessly in my heart for having helped me escape to America despite the ignominy of being in exile and to seek asylum soon. I caught my flight to Detroit, Michigan around 3:45 pm same day.

The Ramseys were at the Detroit Metropolitan International arrivals terminal waiting to receive me. They must have noted the fatigue in my face, if not the sorrow of leaving my beloved Gambia and people behind for an indefinite time.

They welcomed me graciously and we headed for Sandusky, a small village in Michigan. I therein and then became part of the Ramsey family. Life has it that when some of us were created the mould broke. Most give their time and money to their own families or to work that brings them some happiness and some money.

Cloyd Ramsey is among a few who give themselves wholly and unselfishly to others. I can never be able to repay or tell how devoted Ramsey is in sharing life with the needy unless you meet him. In brief, Mr. Ramsey and wife Narrate fed and sheltered me when I needed food and place to stay until I get my feet back on earth.

He was my salvation voice in the wilderness of life's rugged road. I stayed as their guest in Sandusky until it was time to seek asylum at the Immigration and Nationality Service (INS) in Detroit.

There was no other situation less tense and so empty of hope than this next phase in my life. Life became an abyss of despair which only God and good friends, like the Ramseys, pulled me out from underneath. Shakespeare said, between the acting of a dreadful thing and the first motion, all the interim is like a phantasm, or a hideous dream.

The genius and mortals instruments like to a little kingdom, suffers then the nature of an insurrection. Indeed an insurrection has been going on in my head during those horrible days of the coup d'etat of April 15th 1980 I became aware of the need to muster courage, strength and endurance to prepare myself for the coming exile days and form it may take.

Again, Mr. Ramsey contacted the Gambia several time to no avail to verify and correct a possible misunderstanding that may have occurred. Several friends and legislators Ramsey contacted advised that I seek asylum from the INS. Senator Carl Levin sent us a package of three copies of Form 1-589 for my use on 6th January 1982.

We took the bull by the horns, completed the forms and Ramsey and I proceeded to INS office at Mount Elliot Street, Detroit, Michigan on the 22nd February 1982, were I was subsequently interviewed separately and told action will be rendered in four months earliest.

If wishes were horses beggars would gallop to heaven for it took well more than eight months before any reply came and only after numerous INS court hearings did we get some semblance of partial positive direction.

The final act was left with the State Department and vice president's office. Things were so delayed and difficult that I asked Ramsey to take me to the Catholic Mission for me to seek Sanctuary or more public help and support.

We landed at St. Pauls Cathedral, Diocese of Michigan, where Hugh Davis led me to the refugee office of the Diocese. On hearing my story the refugee co-coordinator, Mrs. Patricia Koblinsky called rev. Hugh C. White, advisor to then reigning Bishop of the Diocese, Bishop Coleman Mcgehee Jr.

The Diocese received and let me stay at 44 Ledyard Street in Detroit. In the mean time Ramsey sent the following appeal to the INS office at Mount Elliot in Detroit, Michigan:

TO WHOM IT MAY CONCERN

This letter is to acknowledge my association with Alhasan Ceesay, over a period of fifteen years. During that time I have found him to be a young man of very high ideals. His only interest in life has been to obtain an education and return to serve his home country and help his people.

I have personally invested thousands of dollars in Alhasan Ceesay because it seemed to me to be a very efficient way to help the impoverished people from his country that has had a great deal less than I have. If anyone were to follow the course of his life, he would see that his motives most certainly were not to simply escape the futility of his home country and live that, good life here.

There is no doubt in my mind that the dangers that he describes do exist for him. Even if these were less than perfect proof, would you like to take the chance of being wrong and find out that he had been imprison or worse killed for no reason at all?

Please save this man. If you cannot do it for his sake, then consider the investment made by concerned individuals, other organizations and myself. Thank you for your serious considerations of this matter.

Signed: Cloyd Ramsey, Sandusky, Michigan, USA.

My next Alpena Samaritan and brother in Chris as well as profession was Dr. Charles T. Egli, who I met almost about the same time I did with Ramsey.

He was a Surgeon working for the Medical Arts Clinic at the time of our meeting. He came into the radar after a speech I gave to the Alpena Medical Association. He too has contributed prominently and was instrumental in having the medical Association comes to my aid with a donation of $400 towards my second semester fees at Alpena Community College.

By this miracle I was able to complete payment for the second semester at college. Charles, as he prefers being called, is a surgeon and devoted Christian who also became very close friend and had done a lot to encourage my efforts.

His rallying for assistance continued through out his days at the Medical Arts Clinic. For you to note Dr. Egli's closeness here is a letter he sent in my behalf during my petitioning for asylum in the USA. It read:

Medical Arts Clinic

Alpena, Michigan

November 14, 1986

RE: Deportation Notice on Alhasan Ceesay

Dear Senator Levin,

Alhasan Ceeesay was a college student in Alpena many years ago when I first met him and was very much impressed by his sincerity and enthusiasm. He went onto graduate school at Michigan Technological University in Houghton, Michigan, in hopes of getting into medical school.

He tried very hard to get into medical school in Africa. He was receiving no support from his own country because it considered him a political agitator and tribalist.

Alhasan Ceesay on his own initiative was able to get into medical school in Monrovia Liberia and succeeded in taking two years medical education before he fled for safety to the USA. He later sought political asylum in the USA for fear of persecution due to the aftermath of an attempted coup in July 181.

It has always been his desire to complete his medical training and return to the Gambia when the climate warrants. For almost five years now, Alhasan has been trying to receive asylum, during which time his chances at medical school are affected.

Most recently he received a letter from INS judge ordering his deportation. The deportation of Alhasan Ceesay back to the Gambia would result in his certain death or imprisonment and would constitute another tragedy in the way our government handles people like Alhasan.

In a country where there are so many illegal aliens it seems that there must be some place for one more refugee. I beg you to personally consider Alhasan's case.

Sincerely

Dr. Charles T. Egli, MD

Mr. Homer Shepard, resident of Flint Michigan, was also very kind to me while at Flint. He offered to lodge me during the summer of 1969 on securing a full time job at the St. Joseph Hospital on Flint, Michigan as nurse assistant.

Homer and wife offered to help defray rent expenses, which were taking a quarter of my earnings. With this help I was able to return to Alpena Community College at the end of the summer and pay my dorm and food bills and still had some pocket money to buy pens and other sundries during the semester.

God blesses his heart. We lost contact since my return to Africa. All letters to his address were redirected, as addressee no longer leaves here. Bishop Coleman Mcgehee had already blessed efforts of the hastily formed CEESAY COMMITTEE. It became the adhoc committee and my Pegasus wing.

Like any normal human gatherings we had our different ideas as to how to approach the asylum problem but all of it steered towards or sought better ways to meet the challenges and enigma about to end all that I stood for and worked hard for in life. The brain storming sessions were very pragmatic if not practical and well-intended discussions.

One of the exploratory searches for solutions led us to Mayor Harvey Sloan of Louisville, Kentucky. I met Mayor Sloan in 1976 when I was trying to get into medical school at the University of Louisville.

Also we used to write each other while I was in Monrovia, Liberia, West Africa. I was invited to his office early February 1983, and was given opportunity to talk with key aids at the Louisville City Hall while he attended other state affairs.

His executive aids, Sharon Wilbert and Mrs. Blanche reviewed my case along with information already in my file open in my name. They concluded that I did deserve help and I was asked to speak to Mrs. Joyce J. Rayzer, Director, and Health Affairs for the Mayor. Joyce contacted the Dean of the Medical School and gave him an in-depth briefing of my background and precarious situation I was faced with.

Two weeks later on February 28th 1983, I received the following letter from Joyce in behalf of Mayor Harvey Sloan. It read thus:

Office of the Director of Safety

City Hall

Louisville, Kentucky 40202

28 February 1983

Dear Mr. Ceesay,

It appears, as the old saying goes, that I have good news and bad news. I have been in contact with the University Of Louisville School Of Medicine with regards to your admission at the fall term.

I have spoken to Dr. Donald Kemetz, Dean of the Medical School, and Mr. Harold Adams, Special Assistance to the president of the University of Louisville. Both of these administrators upon reviewing the information you sent me feel that you are a very good candidate for the minority admission program.

There is however, one issue, which must be resolved favorably before your admission to medical school, or the financing and packaging necessary to begging this endeavor can be given serious considerations. The issue, which must be resolved, is the financial determination base on whether you would be granted asylum in the country.

Without the asylum being granted and hence financial aid the university cannot proceed with your request for admission this fall because your legal status would be too tenuous for them to invest hard cash in your future medical development under such nebulous state.

It appears that you must begin medical school anew. The two years completed at Liberia, cannot be accepted for transfer. You will start as freshman upon being granted asylum in USA.

Again, try and find resolution to granting you asylum. I have been assured that everything that can be done for you will be done immediately upon a favorable notice of your asylum. Everybody in the Mayor's office says hello, and we are sending you our prayers.

Sincerely

Joyce J. Rayzer

Director, Health Affairs

This was the impact Mayor Harvey Sloan had. In addition Mayor Harvey Sloan sent the following directly from his desk to the INS pleasing for them to grant me asylum.

City Hall

Office of the Mayor

Louisville, KY 40202

November 7, 1983

Alhasan S. Ceesay of the Gambia has contacted this office in an effort to gain political asylum in other to complete his medical education at the University of Louisville. I know that he is dedicated individual and is more desirous of providing needed medical aid to his fellow man.

Mr. Ceesay petitioned for political asylum in February 22, 1982 due to a purge, which followed a failed coup in the Gambia. The Medical school at the university of Louisville is currently processing his application for the 1984/85 academic years. It would be most helpful if you could assist him in expediting his papers.

He will not be admitted unless a written statement confirming his residency status is available. Since he has already lost two years awaiting residency confirmation, it would be deeply appreciated if you could assist this young man in any way possible. If my staff or I can be any further assistance in the matter, please do not hesitate to contact this office.

Sincerely

Harvey L Sloan

Mayor Louisville

Let us for a moment revert to Bishop Coleman McGehee at the Episcopal Diocese of Michigan in Detroit Michigan. Below is letter sent to the INS director, Edwin Chauvin at Mount Elliot in Detroit Michigan.

Office of the Bishop

4800 Woodward Avenue

Detroit, Michigan 48201

24 October 1983

Dear Mr. Chauvin,

As Bishop for the Episcopal diocese of Michigan, located in Detroit, Michigan, I write you this letter on behalf of Alhasan S. Ceesay, a petitioner for political asylum in the United States. As you may note from the file Mr. Ceesay seeks political asylum base on his fear of political persecution and danger to his physical safety and well being by the government, were he to be returned by the INS to his country the Gambia.

Mr. Ceesay's life will disclose to you, he was active opponent of the political regime in the Gambia. After protesting incarceration of his friends, Mr. Ceesay was placed on a list of individuals who were allegedly involved in criminal activity and who were involved with the

Movement for Justice in Africa (MOJA) and were sought for interrogation by the Gambia government. The Gambia government has singled our Mr. Ceesay because of his political opposition and has prevented him from continuing his medical education in Liberia by cutting off his financial assistance and by asking the Liberian government to return Mr. Ceesay to the Gambia.

I am personally acquainted with Mr. Ceesay, and believe him to be an individual who is worthy of support of the Episcopal Dioceses of Michigan. I feel that it took great courage for Mr. Ceesay to stand up for human rights and to publicly oppose the political regime in the Gambia.

I am convinced that Mr. Ceesay is an altruistic individual who deserves to pursue his medical training to benefit, both in the United States and perhaps elsewhere, those individuals who might be helped by his medical ability. Mr. Ceesay has already establish his medical science aptitude in his studies at Medical School in Liberia, and he has applied to and been accepted by the School of Medicine at the University of Louisville, Kentucky, with tuition to be paid by that institution, upon his authorization to remain in the United States.

Mr. Ceesay has also sought authorization to engage in employment pending the outcome of his asylum request, he proposes to assist in medical research at the university should his employment authorization be granted by your office. Therefore, on behalf of Mr. Ceesay as well as the members of my Diocese, I would urge you to give favorable consideration to Mr. Ceesay's petition and expedite his request for employment and his political asylum petition in every possible way so that his efforts to enter the University of Louisville School of Medicine may not be delayed any longer than may be necessary by legal and administrative procedures which you office follows.

Please feel free to contact me if I can be of any assistance in helping you to reach your determination on this matter. I fervently believed that, upon your investigation of Mr. Ceesay's case, you would reach the conclusions that he would be an asset to the United States, and that his fears as to his persecution and personal safety should he return to the Gambia, have firm foundation in fact.

Very truly yours

(The Rt. Rev.) H. Coleman McGehee, Jr.

Bishop of Michigan

The Bishop of Michigan, H. Coleman McGehee followed the above with a letter to then vice president George Bush Sr. Who sent the following tars reply.

The Vice President

Washington, D. C

April 25, 1984

Dear Rev. McGehee,

Thank you for your recent letter concerning Alhasan S. Ceesay. It was thoughtful of you to write and I appreciate your having taken the time to bring Mr. Ceesay's case to my attention. I have asked the State Department to review all asylum cases and human rights violations, which are brought to my attention.

I have, therefore shared your letter and the enclosures with officials at the Department of State and asked that they review Mr. Ceesay's request and write to you directly. I have also asked that a copy of their response be forwarded to my office. With best wishes.

Sincerely

George Bush

Bishop McGehhee, Bishop Mason, Rev. Hugh C. white, Rev. David Brower, Rev. Bill Woods, Rev. Virgil Jones, and Rev. Mark D. Meyer all touched my heart in similar fashions Hence here is my collective feeling and experience in a nut shell about these devoted men of Christ.

All of the priests lived in Detroit, Michigan except Rev. Mark D. Meyer, who lived in Plane view, Texas, USA. I lived with Rev. Mark Meyer in 1989 after hurricane Hugo devastated our campus at Montserrat, West Indies. The rest of the above I met while trying to defray deportation notice from the INS.

Those were challenging and nerving political moments for m family and I. These men of God never docked when told about my nightmare. These true believers became unique brothers I would like to share few outstanding things they did in style engraved in simple devotion to Christ's dictum.

I write because these men impressed me in their interpretations and devotion to the Gospel of Christ. Hence forgive me if I became a bit sentimental in relaying help they gave to me at various challenging times of my life. They were personal pastors for me.

These were the beacon of hope and faith that stood by me when it was all doom and gloomy for me. They were simple people, humble ones at that, I can confide with, debate with, and had shoulders on which to cry my heart out without being embarrassed and above all expect a little prayer at the end of it. Then guess what? We would be on tract trying to get hold of friends of theirs and people that might lighten my burden.

Their devotion to justice and fairness was magnanimous and are my brothers in Christ. Rev. Mark Meyer, on being told the hardship I endured in Montserrat from hurricane Hugo gave me a room and gifts more than ten thousand US dollars to help me complete my pre-clinics at the American University School of Medicine.

I learnt from these men of God that there is a special strength that can sustain us through almost any difficulty. That strength comes from God and from kind hearts like these Samaritans of good will. The strength comes from partly within but even more, it comes from faith and love of those close to us.

These men gave themselves wholly and as unselfishly to others in need when I met them at the Episcopalian diocese of Michigan. They devoted time to my cause and dropped selfish interests aside to help me fight my case against the INS while I was up to my neck in legal and political mud.

I found nothing in these men but admirable integrity, honesty and unswerving commitment to leading life devoted to God, the Bible and in helping the downtrodden. I always feel elated whenever I get chance to speak to these kind hearts from afar. Meeting them makes me feel reunited with my best friends. I rather have a million more like then than multimillionaires that do not care about the plight of the common man.

Again, I applaud contribution and friendship these men touched my heart and life with. God blesses them. My family, villagers and I are extremely indebted to them. These men translated their concerns, and love of humanity and continued to be my good Samaritans and a bridge over trouble waters.

These believe in the worthiness and sanctity of life. And above all they ascribe to the power of knowledge and justice over ignorance. We look forward to the day we can serenade them amongst us in the smiling coast of the Gambia. We pray they keep fit to be able to join us in the opening ceremony of the Manding Medical Centre at Njawara village, the Gambia, West Africa.

These men translated their deep faith, concerns, and love of humanity. I opted to do my clinical rotations in Colchester, Essex, UK in 1990 and chanced to meet the Robinson's. Keith Robinson vested my newly born baby girl, Famatanding Ceesay, at the Colchester County Hospital, which marked our first meeting.

This slightly shy bloke impressed me a lot. He was all smiles and fund. He titled the little ears of my daughter and told her not to be as bad as her daddy. We all laughed over it. We from that moment liked each other and he became one of my inseparable unique Brits. Keith and wife would visit the Gambia and my girls loved them to bits.

Not for the presents he takes to them each time but because of his amiable personality, altruistic, very caring human he is. He had spent boxes of monetary aid towards my NGO, Manding Medical Centre at Njawara village, and the Gambia.

On the forming of the Friends Manding Charitable Trust, he was unanimously voted chairman of the charity by the members. He had since inspiration of the Friends of Manding Charitable Trust worn the cap admirably and did a job well done for the charity. Also he had been instrumental in the Gambibazaar held every fortnight in Colchester to help raise funds for Manding Medical Centre's goals back in the Gambia.

He is committed to seeing the center come to fruition for the villagers of the Gambia and any that would need its service. Personally, he and his wife had been my lifeline and support. They have always come to my aid the call of expectation and I remain profoundly grateful to him and his wife Lorna V. Robinson.

Ten years ago I was on the verge of preparing becoming a consultant and return to serve the Gambia. Today an untold anguish my life went through in these years was dampened by kindness of Lorna and Keith Robinson and many other kind and generous Brits. They are my Colchester Samaritans and Njawara villager's angels with golden hearts.

We are working hard to seeing that manding Medical center transcends the dream it was to reality for the Lower Badibou region. Its service is much needed by the villagers. God blesses their hearts.

In Manchester many helped but few match Elhaj Asfaque Ahammed, Neville Brown, Kofi Awudo and Ahmed Nizami. Asfaque Ahammed is proprietor of Punjab Collection located at Wilmslow Road in Manchester. A lot has already been revealed about the kindness and generosity of this gentile heart and family in my first book, "The legend again all odds."

Asfaque Ahammed has since my early days in Manchester to today been benevolent towards me. He gives me food and money any time he thinks or feels that I am on the brink of collapsing because of joblessness, hunger, and worries about the state of my equally beleaguered family back home. Only God can reward such humble good people.

Neville and I first met in Montserrat, West Indies while I was a medical student at the American University of the Caribbean. We have ever since been cordial and upon finding me out in Manchester he had steadfastly kept that friendship ablaze.

He in various ways would come to my aid with small but significant donations at the time. He even helped me in securing a job at Belfry House Hotel at Hands Forth in

2006. He is kindhearted fellow and my Montserrat. Kofi Awudo is Toggles gentleman I also met through his link with Neville Brown. He turned to be very kind and generous to me. He bought me shoes and shirts to allow me start work at the above hotel.

Years later on my return from Glasgow, Scotland he was the one that lodged me free of charge for three winter months. He is of exceptional quality and humane person. I remain grateful both fellows.

I met Mr. Ahamed Nizami in 2008, an angel in human flesh, at waseem's work place in Manchester. This lawyer turned Editor and I gelled from that hour to today. He is currently the Chief Editor of the Khalish Magazine, an Urdu language magazine in UK and worldwide. He also doubles as one of the Pakistani group leader in Manchester.

On knowing my predicaments his benevolence surfaced. There nod then he promised to help me with some the problems pulling me down and also indicated interest in helping my NGO Manding Medical Centre get financial aid to get a head start on the provision of its goals for the villagers.

In addition he proposed a fun raising idea using his medium and other avenues that may come to light. We tentatively initiated, depending on approval and provisos set by Keith Robinson, Chairman of Friends of Manding

Charitable Trust in Colchester been met, formation of the Manchester manding Medical Center Annex to be office at 9 knowley Street in Manchester. To further demonstrate his kindness and interest in my goal Ahmed Nizami donated fees for all three PLAB exams I took in 2009.

A few more gentle hearts like Ganem Hadied and Mahmud Adam felt sorry that my life became an unkind and rough ride for me. He said, "Ceesay, I wish I can help more to get you out of the limbo you found yourself. Just believe in God and this pain will one day pass like history."

Mahmud Adam also marched Ganem's effort by collecting money from the Liverpool mosque. Both monies were used for my exam fees and for which kindness I remain eternally grateful to all donors. Mohamed Salam of Greenhey business in Manchester was another Good Samaritan that came to my aid when I was left to sleep in cold weather at Alexandra Park.

Upon contacting him he kindly offered me room in one of his flats in Manchester. He was very kind and generous towards me. We have many times prayed together for my eventual breaking out of nightmarish bad luck life had been to me in recent times. Last but not the least is Sami Bati from Algeria who I stayed with at 245 Great Western Street and who relentlessly called and ask people and friends to come to aid. He raised a bundle to help me pay school fees for my daughters in the Gambia and feed my bones. My brother Abdoullah Hashim and wife Asiya Qadri were very kind Bangladesh cum Pakistani couple I met during the most challenging times of my life.

Their kindness is yet to be matched by their peers. I met the couple while sleeping rough in the street of Manchester as Mohamed Salam' offer of a place came to an abrupt end. The place was rented to a family leaving me homeless with no place to go except spend the nights at cold and treacherous Alexandra Park. It was very risky but being jobless it was the only option left to me.

Hence, it was a miracle when this God fearing Good Samaritan couple came to my rescue. They not only lodged me temporally at their other flat at 2 Sway field in Manchester but also continued to shower me with gifts and food. I certainly look forward to hosting and having my villagers and family serenade this unusually kind and generous couple from Bangladesh.

Yankuba Samateh and dear friend Abdal Nasser deserve a mention with gratitude and thanks for kindness and generosity they showered me with during these dark days and for constantly reminding me that I am more than capable of bringing my dream to fruition for the villagers.

Mrs. Roheyata Corr-Sey, a cousin, remained the most supportive and one that kept encouraging me more than any family member had done during this sojourn of mine. God blesses her and her family.

I look forward to being able to thank her in person for insisting that blood is thicker than water and for being with me in thick and thin of this murderous trail. I just have to have continued faith; confidence to do it and the universe will cooperate to justify these days difficulty.

My life being as mythical as Pelebstine fever, it was full of ups and downs and again it was Ahamed Nizami who offered to lodge me when I was asked to leave my previous address where I was renting. His kindness is phenomenal and transience's mortals. I look forward to him being my guest in the Gambia.

Worth mentioning is Abdullah Shahim, a young Bangladeshi fellow who practiced his believe that we are all God's children and do need to help the miskin whenever we can.

He has graced my life with kindness and brotherhood that any human being yearns to get. He and his wife Asiya Padri have been one of the bright experiences of my UK sojourn. God bless their hearts. Asiya is a shining beauty and sunshine of Abdullah Shahim.

Each day became a specific thrill that lead to that exhilarating moment of victory for mankind. It was a hard challenge and a march placed before me. It is a march I will pursue towards the day I would once again be able to serve the Gambia as a physician.

Friends such as Lorna Robinson, Eliza Jones, Mahmud Adam, Ganem Hadied, Abdinnisir, Faisal, Yusuf Ali, Ishfaque Ahmed, Ahmed Nizami, Abdullah Shahim, and countless angels all suffered my pain and fell through way into my heart through compassion as I plied through financial inadequacies.

Angels like Faisal, Abdal Rhaseed, Abdinnisir, Yusuf Ali, and Mahmud Adam deserved to be classed as paragons of kindness. These Somalis are among many who refused to let me bit the dust because of foot dragging visa problem. They encouraged by sharing food and they had with me and made certain that I persevere for a bright day for family and country.

These are people who help lift my feet when my wings could not remember how to fly away from hardship. Faisal Alim would on weekends prepare hot and well spiced Spaghetti and meat, or buy food for me from the next door restraint.

Abdinnisir Hassan in almost tearful manner would push me into going to get food. On top of this generosity these folks let me stay in their flat at 284 Great Western Street,

Manchester while my lawyer fight not only to untangle but to get the Home office act on change of status request I made to that office back in 2004.

I feel favored, if not blessed having to face these inhuman challenges without losing my sanity. Being in the belly of a ferocious beast is more comfortable than life I am currently saddled.

I feel like being at the interface between Purgatory and hell on earth. Simply put, my experience was no domain for the weak. The dilemma in this life remains ceaselessly changing. These few, this band of altruistic brothers kept me going through many a dark hour of my life in America and Great Britain.

They stood tall for me among many in caring for the plight of those who they never met in poverty stricken parts of the world. Friends like these are angels who lift us to our feet when our wings have trouble remembering how to fly. In this almost inhospitable life friends like these are a great gift indeed.

Tinged with trepidations for what the future can sing I picked up courage and inspiration knowing that good comes out of fighting for what one believes in. Life has taught me how to look after myself and that things do not just happen, people make it happen.

And so the villagers and I appeal for your help and participation with Manding Medical Centre. Together we can walk on water and make this dream of providing medical aid to villages become worthy cause for generations.

I have learnt not to rest on my oars else I fall into a deep and turbulent sea of troubles. I have to keep running in order to be with the best or where I am. I will continue to not only learn to improve my performance but to work hard to see that this dream of providing a much needed medical aid to villagers is brought to fruition.

Dalliance said, "Say of me what you will and the morrow will judge you, and your words shall be a witness before its judgment and a testimony before its justice. I came to say a word and I shall utter it. Should death take me ere I give voice the morrow shall utter it. That which alone I do today shall be proclaimed before the people in the days to come."

Chapter 34

I REST MY CASE

Paul in a letter to Timothy 2 said, "I have fought a good fight, I have finished my course, and I have kept the faith." I hand this work for publication for you to be judge of the ravages of the years and how my life was that of extreme ups and downs.

In reality, I am very grateful to God even though my life met with various misfortunes, the most unbearable being the delay in my becoming a physician.

My life as witnessed in these pages was an assembly of trials and tribulation emanating from roadblocks placed on my path by inhuman laws and unfortunate dark circumstances.

Life has taught me to submit to divine decrees, whatever they may be from God.

I feel on the whole overly rewarded and delivered even though I had no family here in England nor was I as lucky as others who can feel and experience the warmth of their wives and children on daily basis. I succumbed to it as the way things were going to be for me and lived with this state of affairs while in Manchester, England.

I experienced various turns of fate, enough for ten elephant loads, while on the little moat of the silver sea called England.

With my travels I was able to see Europe, the Americas and have learnt a great deal from it as well as experienced numerous unforeseen adventures thrown on my path.

My life in England was pain; fear of deportation, hunger, extreme poverty due to joblessness, solitude and missing my wife and children I loved dearly. I had a huge sense of duty in relation to the villagers and was not ready to fail them because of personal comfort or pleasures.

Consequently Manding Medical Centre and benefits to be accrued from it became my most if not the only occupation and direction in life. Here is Manding Medical Centre if managed well it will do justice to rural health service for the next generation of Gambians to build upon.

The medical centre is now a recognized charity in both the United Kingdom and America. I am committed to serve the villagers so that life of the children and young people would be better than mine when I was young. I hope Manding Medical Centre becomes a model testimony of the boy from Njawara village who doggedly struggled to become a doctor and despite various twists of life is able to provide medical aid and service to villagers in rural Gambia.

May be this will strengthen some other fellow to strive to do better than I did to bring health and happiness to the region.

I hope my adventure persuades youngsters that man is capable of a lot more than he thinks he is capable of. Our footprints must be inspirational to give heart to new coming Gambian generations.

Twenty years ago none would dream of thinking me becoming an author or to challenge powers as I did in this little frame and life of mine. I met a beautiful Maraka girl while I was in Monrovia, Liberia, West Africa. Fatou Koma is daughter of Elhaj Ansuman Koma and Jalian Ture of Kindia from Guinea Conakry.

Her positive attitudes towards me lead our meeting on weekends at Cousin Sainabou Jobe's home. We started going out together and very soon I had the courage to ask her hand in marriage. There was no bone of contention with regards for my love for her. She was the darling of my heart at first sight and I was not going to let a fly land on her from that day onwards. We had a simple wedding because her father did not quite approve of me because of fear for his uneducated but very pretty daughter being dump at one stage of the marriage for another educated city girl.I, in the long run, allied his fears and he ended up being one of my best friends and confidants I had up to the day he went to his maker.

Wife Fatou Koma-Ceesay and I are blessed with three beautiful daughters, namely princesses Famatanding Ceesay, Binta Ceesay, and Roheyata Ceesay. All of who, unlike me, had their schooling start at the age of five.

The elder girl is aspiring to become a doctor and had been admitted to start her premed courses at Alpena Community College in Alpena, Michigan, USA.

Together Fatou Koma-Ceesay, the children and I went through all the tragedy of hunger, poverty and other sad experiences my sojourn in the quest of the Golden flees for the villager brought to us.

Fatou Koma-Ceesay initially hated Manding Medical Centre for she felt it consumed me and took me away from her and the children. The call got me entangled in a web of unfortunate circumstances and laws.

The marriage had at one point almost spiralled to its end as wife' move became questionable. Nonetheless she remained a good mother and wife who took care of the girls in my absence. My mother in-law was battered by confusion and as to why Fatou stuck it out with me under such immense hardship. Love is stronger glue!

We loved each other and so we were able to stand by the other in good or bad times and my trip to England was the worse ever in our connubial life. It caused great turbulences in the marriage but I stuck with it for love's shake and the children who I love dearly. Today, we are back together as family under the same roof while planning and supporting future of our darling girls. God bless Fatou Koma-Ceesay's heart and be reassured of endless love I have for her. For now Dalliance said it best for me when he said, "Say of me what you will and the morrow will judge you, and your words shall be a witness before its judgment and a testimony before it justice.

I came to say a word and I shall utter it. Should death take me ere I give voice; the morrow shall utter it. That which alone I do today shall be proclaimed before the people in days to come." I wrote with the hope the life enshrined herein will serve not only as an inspiration to the despondent but a lesson never to allow this sort of experience it passed through this planet.

I wrote in the hope that life enshrined in my books will serve not only as an inspiration to the despondent and downtrodden but a lesson never to allow this sort of experience it passed through this planet.

I wrote because I felt that my life has something worth revealing to the world to engender tolerance and understanding between people and their governments.

I risked revealing today for all of us to learn from it and move to a better and rewarding future. Among the forces of life is one that stands a certain lofty peak a few is endowed with or able to explore its heights. Ambition urges us to leave the lower surface of earth where the ordinary people live and ascend to heights that pierce the heavens.

This mission has led to numerous Erie paths but for me this Pell-mell towards a better medical service for the neglected villager was a worthwhile adventure. I am profoundly grateful and indebted to my wife Fatou Koma-Ceesay and our daughters, princesses Famatanding Ceesay, Binta Ceesay and Roheyata Ceesay for enduring all the pains that we went through in thick and thin times during my sojourn to America and England.

Also my deepest gratitude goes to Cousin Yata Sey-Corr for helping keep my family hopeful. God bless her heart eternally. I forgive my own brothers and sisters who refused to cater for my family in my absence. Hello, hats off to Sey kunda!

Chapter 35

MY ENDEARING LIFE & FATE

For a while in my native innocence all I had was erudition and wit, which always misfired. Everything I touched came to nothing but failure, whatever I tried to achieve came crashing down on my head.

At any given moment some mishap befalls me and nothing surprised me anymore. I took my current plight with stride and smiled as fate taunts me. I remain poor but my in extinguishable strong will enabled me face life squarely and took me through these dark days.

The twist of fate abated but my age had advanced beyond retrieval. The above apocalyptic life is indeed trying moments for my family and me. The only passion I have is providing medical service to villagers through Manding Medical Centre. My dream spawns better future health service for future generations.

I never set to write a bestseller but to inform and share ideas. Also I enjoy reading it as it is not found in any bookstore. It is hoped that in writing another will be spared of experienced I endured before being able to provide medical service/aid to Gambian villagers.

Browse: http://friendsofmandinggambimed.btck.co.uk or contact alhasanceesay@hotmail.com

To view/purchase books: amazon.com Dr. Alhasan Ceesay books.

DR. ALHASAN SISAWO CEESAY, MD

Mrs. Dado Bah, Dudou's darling, Njawara 2016

Chapter 36

ABOUT THE AUTHOR

I was born at Njawara Village, Lower Badibou District in the North Bank of the Gambia. I am a scion of a Mandinka and Fulani tribe and am one of five siblings. I had my education at Kinte Kunda, then Armitage High School, ending up as a registered nurse at the Royal Victoria Hospital, Banjul, before embarking to the USA on my medical degree quest.

I graduated from the American University School of Medicine in Montserrat, West Indies, in 1992 and returned to the Gambia to start setting up a self-help village health NGO Manding Medical Centre. The Gambia Government and the Badibou local authority register NGO Manding Medical Centre. The centre has treated more than 9000 patients free.

I am married to Fatou Koma-Ceesay and we are blessed with three beautiful girls, Famatanding Ceesay, Binta Ceesay and Roheyata Ceesay. Unlike me, all of them started school early without the roadblocks I had to cross in my early years. I am currently a medical officer at the Royal at the Royal Victoria Hospital on study leave.

It is my hope that this work will inspire others and bring much needy help to providing medical service to rural Gambia. You are urged to log onto: http://friendsofmandinggambimed.btck.co.uk or www.publishkunsa.com to learn more about my work with villagers.

Miss Famatanding Ceesay, Brusubi, Gambia

Have your manuscript become a book by submitting it for possible publication to acquisitions publishes Kunsa. Com

Please contact us to expose your work globally.

PUBLISH KUNSA.COM

Why Publish Kunsa?

At Publish Kunsa.com writers can get published free of all common hassles from soft paperbacks, hard cover to e-book versions.

 Easy to Publish
Etiam ullamcorper. Suspendisse a pell entesque dui, non felis.

 Leave a Legacy
Etiam ullamcorper. Suspendisse a pell entesque dui, non felis.

 Scholarships
Etiam ullamcorper. Suspendisse a pell entesque dui, non felis.

 Worldwide Distribution
Etiam ullamcorper. Suspendisse a pell entesque dui, non felis.

 Donate
Etiam ullamcorper. Suspendisse a pell entesque dui, non felis.

 Excellent Support
Etiam ullamcorper. Suspendisse a pell entesque dui, non felis.

More about Publish Kunsa

Web design by Swinson Web Design

© 2012 Publish Kunsa